INNOCENT TRUTHS &
GUILTY LIES

SHANNON SPRUILL

ISBN: 978-1732023475

For my Family Esau, Derek, Patrick & Brian (forever in our hearts)
Special Thanks to Raquel Thrist
For Naming our Main Character

SAVANNAH TAYLOR

I felt like I was floating on a cloud. I just closed my eyes and embraced the euphoric feeling. I hovered over mountains, and I could see the mountain tops. I took a deep breath and just enjoyed the rhythm of the ride. I did not want this trip to end. When I took these trips, I did not have a care in the world. It was just me and the clouds. Here I could be me. No pretenses and no trying to please anyone. Just me being me. Being me was all I wanted. There were no pressures of life. No worrying about who approves of me or who likes me. Here I did not mind the isolation, and I did not feel lonely. I was at a complete and total peace. Coming down from these trips were the worst. Back to reality and back to dealing with people. I came back and realized that someone was banging on my door. I was sitting on the floor beside my bed. I picked up my paraphernalia and put it in my nightstand drawer next to my bed.

I yelled, "I am coming!" Before I walked out of my bedroom, I turned and surveyed the room to make sure none of my paraphernalia was left out. I proceeded to the front door. I looked out the peephole to see my sister, Nina. I was not in the mood for her judgmental attitude. I opened the door. "Hey, Nina! What's up?"

"So you are not inviting me in?" I moved aside and gestured for her to come in. "Damn girl, you look a hot mess. Were you sleeping?"

"Yes, I was asleep." She was surveying the room like a detective.

"Why are you sleeping on a Saturday afternoon in the middle of July? On a beautiful summer day like today, you should be out and about." She was beginning to piss me off.

"Listen, I will do with my day what I want. Now, what did you come over here for because we both know that this is not a social call?"

"Well, I was doing mom a favor and dropping off this package to you from her. Here it is, and I guess I will be leaving." She turned and pranced out the door. She did not bother closing the door behind her, so I went and shut it.

Nina and I never got along. She is younger than me and was always jealous of me. She felt like our parents put me on a pedestal and I was their favorite. I don't believe I was the favorite, but I worked hard to accomplish my goals, and that made them proud. Unlike me, Nina never applied herself because she was so busy being a little miss social butterfly. I honestly felt like Nina hated me. When I was around 7 years old, I remember we were at camp and we were at the pool. I was afraid to go in the pool for fear of drowning. Nina snuck up behind me and pushed me in the deep end of the pool. The lifeguard had to jump in and save me. We never had a close sister relationship. She was waiting for me to fail and disappoint our parents.

One thing that she was right about, I needed to get out of this house. I almost forgot about the package. I knew what it was before I opened it. I was admiring a sweater that my mother was wearing, and she promised to get one for me. I opened the package and as I thought there was a beautiful lavender colored sweater in the box. Glad Nina did not know what was in the box.

When I am not taking trips, I work at a private law firm, and I am a criminal defense attorney. I am the only woman in the firm and the men challenge my skills daily. I believe the fact that I am African American does not help. I catch a lot of flack because the rumor is Bill is considering me for a partner. William Winston, Bill, is one of the partners and has been a fan of mine from the day I started working at the firm. It is hard working in the all-boys club, but I will not let them stop me from making partner. The Law Office of Winston and Cicarelli will become the Law Office of Winston, Cicarelli and Taylor. That would shut so many mouths. In 10 years I have not lost a case, and I think that is what gets under the skin of my colleagues.

I think my success also gets under the skin of my sister. My sister is two years younger than me. As young children, we always fought with one another. I love my sister, but for some reason, the feeling is not mutual. I tried to have a heart to heart with her a few years ago, but the conversation went south very quickly. She always complained that I was our parent's favorite, and I was nothing but a loser hiding behind the praise that our parents poured out. I never really understand the root of her resentment, and I just stopped trying to figure it out. She took delight in my failure, and if she knew about the trips I took, she would use that to destroy me.

I live alone even though I have a boyfriend. His name is Danny, and we have been dating for five years even though we have known each since grammar school. We have a unique relationship. There is no pressure, and we give each other space. It works for the both of us. With all of my success, something was missing in my life, and I could not put my finger on it. I was not completely happy or was I using the thought of unhappiness as an excuse to take my trips. I got out of the house and went to Central Park.

I enjoyed going to the park and people watching. I got a hot dog and a Pepsi and spent the next couple of hours just watching people. When I got home later that evening, I went on another trip. I usually took about 2 to 3 trips a

4

day. I was what you would call a functioning drug addict. It started out as a curiosity, and it is now a full-blown addiction. Yes, I do realize that I am a drug addict and no I don't need help. I have my addiction under control. I enjoy getting high, and I am not hurting anyone in the process. I support my habit and don't forget, I am a very successful attorney. I do not get high with anyone. When I take a trip, it is my secret addiction.

As I was coming down from my high, I looked at the television, and there was a late-breaking news report. I turned up the television to hear the story. IBF, WBA and IBO world heavyweight champion, Dante Jackson has been arrested for suspicion of murder. It turns out Dante is accused of killing his live-in girlfriend. Wow, this was big news because Dante was supposed to be the next Muhammad Ali. I changed to a different channel, and as I thought, all the major networks were carrying the report. That is a great career down the toilet. I did not know all the details, but I felt sorry for him.

My cell phone started ringing. "Hello."

"Hey Savannah, I am sure you saw the late-breaking news. We will be representing Dante Jackson, and this is going to be your case. I know tomorrow is Sunday, but can we meet for lunch and I can brief you on what I know so far?" Bill did not waste any time jumping all over this one. A lot of our clients were NBA and NFL players, so this did not surprise me that we would be representing a boxer.

"Yes, we can meet for lunch around 1 pm. Does that work for you?"

"Yes, that is perfect. We can meet at Matto Espresso on Columbus Avenue."

That was perfect for me because I live at 730 Columbus Avenue in the Westmont Apartments and Matto is located at 530 Columbus Avenue.

"Perfect, see you tomorrow." I decided to turn in early because I did not want to be tempted to take another trip.

I got to Matto before Bill did, so I went and got a table for us. This case could be the most significant case of my career. So it is crucial for me to make sure that I get this right. Bill arrived about five minutes after I did.

"You weren't waiting too long?" Bill always seems to be in a hurry.

"No, I just got here about 5 minutes ago." I was really interested in hearing about this case.

"Are you going to order some food?"

I was not hungry because I had taken a trip right before coming here. "No. I just got some coffee." I was ready to hear about this case.

"I guess you heard most of the details on the news regarding Dante. We will be representing him, and you will be taking the case."

"Are you sure you want me on this case? This will be one of our biggest cases. Do you think he is innocent?"

"Yes I want you on this case, and I don't care if he is innocent or not. It is your job to convince the jury that he is innocent. His arraignment is tomorrow." I believe Bill never cares about the true innocence of our clients. He is fixated on winning at all cost.

"I will meet with him before the arraignment to have a quick interview with him. Do you have any details from the crime scene?"

He took a file from his briefcase and opened it. "She was found at his house. Neighbors reported hearing gunshots. When the police arrived at the scene, Dante was not at the house. He claims he was at the park working out. He has no one that can confirm that he was at the park. She was shot once in the head. It had all the makings of a professional hit. That is the only thing that makes me think that maybe Dante is not lying. Where the problem lies is a neighbor swore that she saw Dante leaving the house shortly after hearing the gunshots. Just keep in mind that all eyes are on this case. Dante is the heavyweight champion and so much is at stake. Win this one, and you can write your ticket going forward. I chose you because I have faith in you and I know what you are capable of doing. Don't let me down."

Wow, a great way to put the pressure on me. "I will do my best."

"Your best is not good enough for this one. You need to win this case." All I could think about at this very moment was taking a trip.

Sometimes I wonder why I continued in this business because of the continued stress that I am experiencing. I love and hate my job at the same time. Before I went home, I made a stop to see Devon. Devon supplies me with tickets for my trips. We always meet at a little coffee shop down the block from my house. I have known Devon for years. We went to high school together but took different paths after we graduated. Devon was a low-level drug dealer, and he had a regular clientele, and he did not want to take on any new clients. He was cautious and has never got busted. He was the first person to give me heroin even though he was against it. I was working a difficult case and was under a lot of pressure. We remained friends after high school, and I knew that he dealt drugs. I asked for a hit to take the edge off and relax. He initially said no, but I convinced him to give me a hit. And the rest is history. I don't shoot up; I only smoke. Do I regret my choice? Surprisingly the answer is no. I am not hurting anyone, and I enjoy my trips. It is the way I unwind and relax. When I got to the coffee shop, Devon was already there. I ordered a mocha latte, and we talked for a few moments and exchanged money and drugs.

"Hey, did you hear about Dante Jackson?"

"Yeah I heard, and that case just got dropped in my lap."

"Do you think he did it?"

"I don't know besides I have not talked to him yet. I will meet with him in the morning."

Devon got up to leave. "I wish you luck with that case.

I have to run, so I will check with you later." I also left and went home.

When I got home, the first thing I did was take a trip. For the next 2 hours, I just enjoyed my trip. I grabbed my laptop and Google Dante Jackson. I got a notebook and started jotting down information about Mr. Jackson. I wanted to get a feel for what the public thought of Dante. He was a star athlete with a squeaky clean past. This was the first time that he was in trouble. I could not say the same for his brother Eugene Jackson. Everyone called him Gene, and he was a well-known gang member and drug dealer. He had a long rap sheet. Dante and Gene were close, but Gene respected Dante's choices in life, so he kept him away from his criminal activity. I made a note that I should talk to Gene.

His mother and father live in Queens, and both worked. His father is a sanitation worker, and his mother runs a daycare. Regardless of Dante's success, both parents insisted that they would keep their jobs and stay in their home. I would have to talk to his parents. Next, I wanted to get to know about his girlfriend. Her name was Elyse Daniels, and she had been dating Dante for four years. They were planning to get married next year. Her father was Robert Daniels, and her mother died while giving birth to her. A single father raising a little girl all by himself. Wow, that is brownie points for dear old dad. This case was shaping up to be one of my more difficult ones. I found nothing that was a blemish on Elyse's perfect existence. And it seems that they had an excellent relationship. There was no motive for Dante to kill his girlfriend. That was the one positive about this case, but the neighbor who saw him is a problem. I will have to interview the neighbor. I then asked myself the one question I always ask myself when I take on a new case, "What if he did it?"

2

GETTING TO KNOW DANTE

*D*ante's arraignment was at 10 am, and I got there at 9 am. I wanted to see Dante before the appearance. I waited in a small room for Dante. The room was painted a hospital green, and I felt like I was in some asylum. I was expecting the men in white coats to come through the door with a straight jacket. While I waited, I reviewed the rest of the file. One of the arresting officers was Jeffrey Johnston. Damn, I had not seen Jeffrey since we broke up over five years ago. Our break up was terrible, and because he was a cop, it was hard for me to get help. He was abusive and very possessive. In some sick way, I believe that Jeffrey did love me, but I quickly fell out of love with him when he decided to put his hands on me. I knew it was time for me to get out of the relationship when I started thinking about killing him. When I called the police after he got physical with me, I somehow felt like the criminal, not the victim. He was very manipulating, and his police buddies were happy to cover for him. I got a restraining order, and that did not help because he felt he was above the law.

Bill Winston talked with him, and he suddenly stopped bothering me. I am not sure what Bill said to him, but it worked. When I asked him, he merely said, "remember we work together." I did not know what he meant by that, but I left it alone because I was so happy that Jeffrey was not bothering me any more. By now he must know that I am the defense attorney for this case. I am not looking forward to seeing him in that courtroom.

I could hear feet shuffling and chains clinking as Dante approached the room. He had on handcuffs and chains on his ankles. The officer walked him over to the table where I was sitting. He took another pair of handcuffs and used those to handcuff him to the table. Once Dante was situated the guard left the room, but I could see him through the little window in the door, standing outside. Dante looked calm, and surprisingly he did not look scared. He looked exhausted.

"Hi Dante, I am Savannah Taylor, and I will be representing you. Have they been treating you okay?" As he spoke to me, I noticed that he would not look me in the eyes. He held his head down.

Dante looked away from me as he answered. "They're treating me okay. First thing I want you to know is I would never kill my girlfriend. I loved Elyse, and we were getting married next year. If you're going to represent me, I need you to believe me." He did sound sincere and believable.

"Dante it is my job to make sure that the jury believes you. I will need you to look me in my eyes when talking to me." He slowly raised his head and looked me in the eyes. "Now first I want to go over exactly what happened that night. I need you to give me a step-by-step account and do not leave out any details."

He looked at me for the first time. "Where do you want me to begin?"

"I want you to take me through the whole day from the time you and Elyse woke up that morning."

He set up in his seat. "When I woke up around 8 o'clock that morning Elyse was already in the shower. We both got dressed, and we had a light breakfast together. We watched the news like we do every morning and she left for work. I headed over to the gym to work out for a while. I called her during the day to see what her plans were for dinner and she said she was having dinner with her father. After a workout at the gym, I ran a bunch of errands and went home. When I got home, Elyse was not home yet, so I decided to go to the park and run. After my run in the park, I went home, and that is when I discovered that Elyse was dead. I am not sure when Elyse got home, but it had to be shortly after I left for the park. The only reason I say that is because I wasn't gone more than two hours."

I was expecting to see a little more emotion when he talked about Elyse, but he was very calm. "Do you recall if you saw anyone in the park that would remember seeing you?"

"I do not remember seeing anyone. I had my beats on listening to music as I ran."

"Did you and Elyse argue that day at all or had you argued recently within the last couple of weeks?"

He had a perplexed look on his face. "What couple doesn't argue?" This question seemed to agitate him a little.

"These are questions that the prosecutor will ask, so I am trying to get ahead of the game and make sure there are no surprises." I closed up my briefcase, and I looked Dante in the eyes.

"From this point forward I need you to be sincere and transparent with me. What you tell me is confidential, and you have a lawyer-client privilege. What that means is you have the right to refuse to disclose and to prevent any other person from disclosing confidential communication between yourself and your attorney. If I am going to do my job, I need to know that you are forthcoming. I do not want to be in that courtroom and get caught off guard because you neglected to give me information that the prosecutor can get first.

Now when we go out to your arraignment, the judge is going to ask you how do you plead and you are to say not

guilty. I am going to request bail, but I must be honest there
is a strong possibility that it will get denied. I will arrange
time later after your arraignment for us to meet again and go
over some more of your statement. There is a list of people
that I will be interviewing including family members and the
neighbor who claims to have seen you leaving the apartment
the night of the murder." I stood up and called for the guard.

"I'll see you out in the courtroom."

"Thank you, Ms. Taylor."

When I walked into the courtroom, the first person I
saw was Jeffrey. I could tell that drinking aged him. He
was walking towards me.

"Hello, Ms. Taylor."

"Hi, Jeffrey." He had a very smug look on his face. I just
wanted to move on.

"Looks like you might be headed for your first loss." I
did not want to play this game with him. I just walked to
my seat next to my client. The arraignment went quickly
and like I thought, the judge denied bail. When I found
out that the Judge was Judge Hanna, I already knew it was
going to be hard to get bail. He is known for being a
tough judge. I left the courtroom before I would run into
Jeffrey again and went home.

I needed to take a trip and unwind. Just as I was
enjoying my trip, my phone rang. I knew it was Bill.

"Hi, Bill."

"Hey, Savannah. I was calling to find out how everything went at the arraignment." I guess he was expecting me to come into the office.

"Everything went well. I just thought I could work better from home. I am creating a list of people to interview, so I can start building a character reference for Dante."

"I did not expect you to come into the office. Well, what are your thoughts?" I know what he meant; he wanted to know if I thought he was innocent.

"It is too early to tell." That was not the answer he was expecting.

"You have to have some initial impression."

"It is difficult to tell so early. The only thing that I noticed was there was no emotion when he talked about the murder of his girlfriend."

"He is probably still in shock." Bill had a way of ignoring the obvious to win.

"You might be right. I will update you as I gather more information."

I think I was going to start with Elyse's father. I thought I would get the difficult interview out of the way. In the file, I had a phone number for Robert Daniels. I called the number, and the phone rang five times before he answered.

"Hi, Mr. Daniels. My name is Savannah Taylor, and I am the defense attorney representing Dante Jackson. I have a few questions, and I was wondering if we can meet." There was silence for a few seconds (seemed like a lifetime).

"I guess everyone has a job to do. I don't hate Dante, but I need to know what happened. What I need to know is if he is responsible for killing my baby girl. You have no idea of the pain I am in right now. It hurts so bad, and I miss her so much. She did not deserve this. Sorry for rambling."

"It is ok, and it is understandable. Can we meet this afternoon around 3 pm? I have your address if you will be home or will you be at work?"

"I took a leave of absence from work. I need time to process what has happened. Yes, I can meet with you at 3 pm. I will see you then."

"Thank you and talk with you then." When I hung up, I tried to imagine how he must be feeling and it was impossible for me to comprehend. I know it must be painful, but because I don't have children, I did not truly understand the depths of his pain. I felt terrible that I had to interview him at this time. I would try my best to be courteous and considerate of his feelings. I went on to schedule interviews with Dante's parents and his brother. Finally, I scheduled a meeting with the witness who testified to seeing Dante leaving the murder scene. I needed to get a better take on who Dante Jackson is and is he capable of murder. There is a part of me that feels that in the right situation, everyone is capable of murder.

I finished up my paperwork, made a few appointments, and decided to take a quick trip before going to see Mr. Daniels. After my trip, I took a quick shower and put on a sundress. I always wore a suit when going to court. The sundress was comfortable but still very professional looking. It was 85 degrees and very humid. I was much cooler wearing the sundress. Mr. Daniels lived at 18 Morningside Ave in the new Morningside Park Condominium. I arrived at 2:55 and found a convenient parking spot. His apartment was on the first floor. I rang the buzzer, and he let me in, and there he was in the doorway looking so tired and gaunt. "Mr. Daniels, thank you so much for taking the time to speak with me. I know this is a difficult time for you." He stepped aside and motioned for me to come inside. We walked into his living room, and he motioned for me to have a seat. His place was breathtaking. "Wow Mr. Daniels, did you decorate this place by yourself?"

"Yes, I did. I am domestic, and I love decorating. Elyse was just the opposite. She was a tomboy and loved sports. As you can tell, we were very close. It was not easy raising her on my own but I did the best job a father could do. I was both dad and mom. When she met Dante, she brought him home to meet me. He was a nice enough young man. He was very kind and respectful. When she told me she was moving in with him, I was against it because I am old fashion and I believe in marriage before living together. But my daughter was headstrong, and so she moved in with Dante. On the surface, their relationship seemed great and looked as if they were doing very well. They argued like most couples but nothing earth-shattering."

"Did you know about these arguments?"

"Yes when they disagreed, she came running to me, There were times I had to make her see where she was wrong and there were times that Dante and I talked when he was in the wrong. I grew to love Dante like a son. As a boxer, he did travel a lot, and I hated Elyse being alone. That was the overprotective father in me. There was one odd thing that Elyse told me one time. She said that when he returned from any of his trips, he seemed to be in a dark mood. Not quite depressed but just dark was how she described him. Never thought much of it but I told her it was probably related to his boxing. Now to answer the question I know you probably want to ask me; do I think that Dante is capable of murder? Well, he could be capable of murder, but I thought he would never be capable of hurting my little girl. It seemed like she meant the world to him. If Dante did this, he seriously had me fooled." Mr. Daniels was so forthcoming with information. He did most of the talking. I was starting to form an opinion regarding Dante, but I still had a long way to go to prove his innocence. And the golden question was, who would want Elyse dead?

"Mr. Daniel, I do not want to take up any more of your time and thank you for taking the time to talk with me." I stood up to leave, and he looked at me pleadingly.

"If he did this, I hope he gets the death penalty or life in prison with no possibility of parole. If he did not do this, help him prove his innocence and find out who did this to my baby girl. I am a fair man, and I want the right person to pay for this." Elyse was lucky to have this man as her father.

My next stop was Elmhurst, Queens. I was going to meet with Dante's parents. They were surprisingly not at his arraignment. It took me almost an hour to get to Queens because of the traffic. When I arrived at their house, both Mr. and Mrs. Jackson greeted me at the door. "Good afternoon Mr. and Mrs. Jackson."

"You can call me Bill and my wife is Dianne. Please come in." I followed them into the house, and they led me to a very quaint sitting room.

"Please have a seat. Can you tell my wife and me if you will be able to get our son out of jail."

"A mother knows her child, and I know that Dante would never kill anyone and he loved that girl."

"Bill and Dianne, I am doing my best to represent your son and make sure he gets a fair trial." Dianne Jackson stood to her feet.

"Fair trial? Are you kidding me? They are already convicting him in the media and painting a picture of a monster!" She was visibly upset, and I did not want to make things worse before I had a chance to question them.

"I understand the pain that both of you are experiencing. My job is to paint the picture of who Dante is, and I need your help to do that. I need you to tell me about Dante. What type of person is he? What are his likes and dislikes? This information will be helpful in preparing my opening statement." Dianne sat back down. I need to make her realize that I was on her side.

During our entire conversation, I continued to think about how calm Dante was when he described the murder. That fact did not sit well with me. I listened as they painted this picture of a kid that overcame the odds. He turned to boxing because as a kid he was bullied, and boxing was a way to release his frustrations. He did not drink or do drugs. He was an average student in school. He was the youngest of two. His brother Eugene was one year older than him, and he was the troubled child. This was not the resume of a murderer. I decided to ask more direct questions.

"Has Dante ever seen a psychiatrist?" Both Bill and Dianne looked at each other. There was something here. "It is not a bad thing if he did but I need to get in front of this before the prosecutor goes digging and they will put a negative spin on it. Help me help Dante." Bill spoke up first.

"Yes, Dante saw a psychiatrist for a while. He was dealing with some depression, and he sought help."

"How long ago was this?" He thought for a moment.

"It was during his senior year in high school. He was 17 years old, and we did not know how to help him."

"He is 27 years old so that would have been ten years ago?"

"Yes, that is correct. I am not sure how long he went."

"It is possible that he is currently seeing a psychiatrist?"

"I don't know. Do you think that will hurt his case?"

"No, not at all. But it is important for me to present it before the prosecution has a chance. I will spin it positively. Trust me. Lastly, has Dante ever hurt anyone intentionally?" It was Dianne's turn to speak up.

"Absolutely not. Even though he had bouts with depression, he is a kind and loving person. He would never hurt anyone." I noticed that his father was looking away as if avoiding something.

"Bill, is there something that you want to add?" Dianne looked like she was begging him not to talk.

"Dianne, we have to be totally honest if we are going to help Dante. Dante did hurt a young lady during his senior year in high school. That is what prompted him to start seeing a psychiatrist. It was a young girl that he was dating and there was a rumor that she was cheating on him. He confronted her, and they got into an argument, and he started choking her. He choked her until she lost consciousness and used a knife to cut a small x on her shoulder. The girl recovered, and she was alright, but it was then that he realized he needed help." I looked over at Dianne, and she was crying.

"Dianne, I am glad your husband is honest with me. I

will talk with Dante because I will need for him to sign some forms allowing his doctor to talk with me. Don't worry; we need to be in the driver's seat and not let the prosecutors beat us to the punch. I have taken up enough of your time. I may have additional questions later, but I will contact you in advance." I got up to leave, and Dianne hugged me.

"Please help my son," I reassured her that I would do my best. I had some other things to do, but I needed to go home and take a trip. I would call Bill in the morning and give him an update. On second thought, I would probably go into the office tomorrow.

3

DIGGING DEEPER

I got up early and took a trip. It was 5 am, but I wanted to get a trip in before going into the office. I got to the office around 9:15 am, and Bill was not there, so I decided to get some paperwork done. We had a generic medical release form that I prepared to take with me when I went to visit Dante. Bill got in around 10:30 am and popped his head into my office.

"Hey, Savannah. How is it going?"

"Well, I have to do some damage control. Come in and have a seat." He came in and sat down.

"What's going on?"

"Well, our star boxer has some skeletons in his closet. Looks like he hurt a young lady in his senior year of high school. He choked her unconscious and used a knife to carve a small X on her shoulder. After that, he started seeing a psychiatrist. This information came from his parents. I have not spoken to Dante yet, but I will be going to see him this afternoon. I will have to talk with him and also get information from the shrink before I can figure out how to get in front of this situation." Bill leaned back in his chair and scratched his head.

"Well at this point I am going to let you do your job. I have faith in you and if you need anything, let me know." He stood up and headed for the door. "I would be curious to hear what the shrink has to say. I will check with you in a couple of days."

I decided to drive to the Bronx to see his brother. Dante was at Rikers Island, so I would have time to see his brother before I had to be at Rikers. His brother had an apartment at Noonan Towers, on Woodycrest Avenue. He lived in a nice neighborhood. I rang his apartment doorbell, and he answered. He let me in and led me to the living room.

"So you are the lawyer that is representing my brother. Will you be able to get him out?"

"I am doing my best to get your brother released. Thank you for taking the time to speak with me." He sat down next to me.

"No problem. Besides, he is my brother, and I would do anything for him. He is not equipped to murder anyone."

"Can I ask you one question? Can you tell me anything

about the incident that happened in high school with the young lady that your brother choked? I understand after that he was under the care of a psychiatrist." His brother looked very agitated when I asked this question.

"Why does that have to be brought up? That was in his past and should have nothing to do with this case. You show me one person that hasn't done something and regretted it afterwards. Yes, he made a mistake back then, but he has never done anything like that since then."

"Eugene, it is important for me to know these things before the prosecution can use it to damage your brother's character. I need to know everything good and bad if I'm going to help your brother prove his innocence. I also need to know how often your brother and you hang out together. And I am sure you understand why I am asking that question." I saw the frustration on his face, but I believe Eugene really understood that I was trying to help his brother.

"I spoke to Dante almost every day, but he was never around me in the streets. Dante is a different person than I am and I made sure that I kept him from my business. I am not saying that Dante was perfect because we all have our faults. He could not do what he is being accused of doing."

"I must go because I am scheduled to meet with Dante today. I will contact you if I have any further questions. In the meantime, if you think of anything that is important for me to know, please give me a call and thanks for your time."

I left Eugene's house and headed to Rikers Island. I hated going to the prison and hearing those gates shut behind me. I hated the thought of being locked up and being told what to do. All of your privileges stripped from you. I know that the majority of the men and women behind those bars deserve their punishments, but I think I would be the one that would lose my mind. Sometimes it's hard to cope when you're a free person so I can imagine how it would be difficult as a prisoner. By the time I got to Rikers, it was pouring down rain, thundering and lightning. The weather added to the doom and gloom of Rikers. Once I was checked in, I was led to a waiting room. I waited 40 minutes before he was brought into the room. He sat down, and he looked tired. "Hi, Dante. How are you doing?"

"Under the circumstances, I am doing ok."

"How are they treating you?"

"There are no problems.". He knew what I was asking. I wanted to make sure he was not being abused or mistreated. I pulled out my file.

"Dante you neglected to tell me about the incident in High School and the fact that you are or were seeing a psychiatrist. The prosecution will jump all of this, and I would not have seen it coming. I have to know everything because you must believe that the prosecution will find it and use it against you. Before we talk about that incident, is there anything else you want to tell me?" He took a deep breath before he spoke.

"There were two other girls that my parents did not know about." This was not good.

"What happened to them?"

"I had anger management issues. I saw a doctor that helped me with getting my anger under control. Both incidents were me losing control and resorting to physical force."

"How bad were they hurt?"

"They were not hurt badly, and I was forbidden to be within 100 feet of them. They had restraining orders against me. I'm sorry I did not tell you this in the beginning and I hope this does not hurt my case. That is everything." Dante has made my job a little harder.

"Did you use a knife on these young ladies?" There was a look in his eyes that I could not put my finger on. "Remember I need the truth." He dropped his head before answering.

"Yes I did use a knife."

"Dante I will need to talk to your doctor and get his assessment. I will need you to sign this release form." He hesitated before signing the document. "Is there something wrong Dante?"

"No, it is just sometimes he and I didn't see eye to eye." I had a bad feeling, but I needed to talk to the doctor first.

"Dante I will need to talk to the doctor, and we will talk after," I called for the guard and prepared to leave.

"Ms. Taylor I'm sorry I was not honest in the beginning but I still hope that you believe in me." It was getting harder to believe in Dante and that was making my job difficult.

4

WHAT OTHERS SAY

*B*efore I went to see Dr. Benginger, I needed to take a trip. Unfortunately, I did not have time to drive home before my meeting with the doctor and that usually meant I would be a little edgy. The doctor's office was located in the Bronx. Today he was working out of Bronx Psychiatric Center. I was confident I could hold it together long enough to interview the doctor. I got to his office at 4 PM and his waiting room was empty. The receptionist at the front desk was very pleasant.

"I have an appointment with Dr. Benginger and my name is Savannah Taylor."

"He is expecting you and I'll let him know that you are here. Just have a seat and I'll let you know when he's ready to see you." I usually carry a ticket with me for emergency situations, but I didn't this time and I was really regretting it. I was hoping that I would not have to wait too long because I really needed to take a trip. I waited five minutes before she came out to let me know that the doctor was ready to see me.

"You can come right this way, Dr. Benginger will see you now." When I entered his office, he stood to greet me.

"Good afternoon, Ms. Taylor. Please have a seat." I really wanted to get right to the point without sounding like I was in a hurry.

"Thank you for taking time to speak with me. Here is the medical release form that was signed by Dante Jackson. You are aware that he has been accused of murdering his girlfriend. I just need to get to know more about the character of Dante." He sat up in his chair and rubbed his chin.

"Are you asking if I think he is capable of murdering his girlfriend?"

"Well, if you wish to get straight to the point, yes do you think he is capable of murder." He pondered my question for a few moments.

"I think in the right situation, everyone is capable of murder. I know you are privy to Dante's temper and some incidents where he has lost control. Yes I believe Dante is capable of murder but I do not believe he murdered his girlfriend. You have a surprised look on your face. Dante came to me with anger management issues but his problems go deeper than that. Dante requires structure and order in his life when it pertains to women. Where there is no structure or order, Dante can spiral out of control. I believe his girlfriend brought structure and order into his life."

"But could something have happened that night that went against the structure and order she brought?" He thought about my question for a few moments before answering.

"She was special and I think in Dante's mind she could do no wrong. Now if he was accused of killing another woman I would not be so quick to defend Dante. He could lose control with another woman because in his mind no other woman could live up to his girlfriend. You have to also understand that Dante's mind does not work like yours and mine."

"So are you saying that he is crazy?" He chuckled and sat up in his chair.

"In my profession, we do not use the word crazy. Let just say that Dante has some mental challenges." In my world that sounds a lot like crazy. I was not sure what to think.

"Ms. Taylor, trust me Dante did not kill his girlfriend."

"I appreciate that but I still have to convince a jury. Would you be willing to testify on his behalf?"

"Of course I would testify if needed. I am sorry but I do have another appointment I need to get to." I stood up to leave.

"Thank you so much for your time. I may have additional questions later." The good doctor escorted me out of his office. I wanted to visit the eyewitness next but I need to go home and take a trip. I would make her my first appointment in the morning. I also thought about visiting Dante tomorrow but I decided to wait until I gather more information and piece some things together. Tomorrow was Friday, so my revised plan would be to visit Dante on Monday. I will also give Bill an update after visiting with the eyewitness.

When I got home, I did not hesitate before going on a trip. I was so relaxed and zoned out that I did not realize that my phone was ringing. I did not want to answer it but I was one of those people that thought every phone call must be important. After I answered it, I was sorry I did.

"Hello."

"Hey big sis! I see you landed a very high profile case. How does it feel to be in the spotlight once again?" Nina was drunk and I was not in the mood. Nina has a drinking problem and denies it. When she gets drunk, I am always her sounding board. But this time, she was blowing my high.

"Nina, I am busy and I don't have time for this."

"Yeah! Miss bigshot! You are always looking down on others like you better than everyone."

I did not say a word. I just hung up the phone and turned off the ringer. I enjoyed the rest of my trip. I made a mental note to give Danny a call tomorrow. We have not spoken in two weeks. It was a little strange that he did not call. I know he must have heard about Dante and he still did not call. I was not overly concerned because honestly speaking we were drifting apart and I was not sure if I was in love with him anymore or if I ever was. I was definitely not going to lose any sleep over it. I pulled out my file to review the information on the eyewitness. Her name was Lana Morgan and she was 68 years old. Her house was diagonal from Dante's. She lived in that house for 28 years. The one thing I found disturbing was the fact that after her statement was taken, no one interviewed her. Usually a detective would follow up with an eyewitness but there was no records of anyone following up with Mrs. Morgan. She was a widow. Her husband died 6 years ago. Well I would see what Mrs. Morgan has to say in the morning because right now I just wanted to go to sleep. I took a nice hot and steamy shower and went straight to bed.

When I woke up, I felt good. I took a trip and put an emergency ticket in my purse. As I was about to leave my phone rang.

"Hello."

"Hey Savannah. I wanted to know if we could meet later to talk. Is 4 pm good for you?" It was Danny and I had a feeling that this would be the goodbye conversation.

"That is fine. You can stop by my place around 4.

Talk to you then." I did not bother to ask what he wanted to talk about because honestly, I did not care.

Dante lives in Sag Harbor, New York. He could definitely afford it but not the place where I thought a boxer would settle down. Sag Harbor is part of South and East Hamptons. The homes in Sag Harbor were amazing. Dante's house was located in East Hamptons. It was a nice drive and driving through the neighborhoods in Sag Harbor was so relaxing. I pulled up into Mrs. Morgan's driveway. She was standing in her doorway waving at me. She looks like she is seventy years old and a busy body. I could imagine her getting into everyone's business. As I approached her, she opened the screen door.

"You must be Ms. Taylor."

"Yes I am and thank you for taking time to talk with me." I stepped into her beautiful home and followed her through the house and out the back door.

"I thought it would be nice to sit on the deck. It is nice to meet you. I don't get many visitors since my husband died." I sat down and took out my notepad. I really wanted to get to the point with Mrs. Morgan, because I could tell that she was lonely and a talker.

"Mrs. Morgan, can you tell me what you saw on the night of the murder at Mr. Jackson's house?"

"I was sitting in my living room watching Judge Judy. I tape all the judge shows because I love watching those and Judge Judy is my favorite. She can get on my nerves sometimes but I love her. Would you like something to drink?" I decided not to rush her and I let her talk.

"Yes I would like a glass of water if you don't mind." She got up and went inside and brought out a pitcher of ice cold water.

"Now back to that night. As I was watching Judge Judy, I suddenly heard a gunshot."

"How did you know it was a gunshot?" She had a puzzled look on her face.

"I know what a gunshot sounds like. Besides, there was a dead girl who was shot." I was not sure if she was being sarcastic but I continued.

"Tell me about who you saw leaving the house after the gunshot."

"It was Mr. Jackson."

"Can you describe what he was wearing?" She thought for a few seconds before answering.

"He had on dark pants and a jacket with a hood."

"What color was the pants and jacket?"

"He was too far away for me to make out the exact color of his clothing."

"Well if you could not make out the color of his clothing, how were you able to tell that it was Mr. Jackson?"

"I know it was him. I am almost positive." Almost positive was not going to cut it and I doubt she knew who she saw.

"What is your vision Mrs. Morgan?"

"My vision is 20/400 but I can see very well."

"Last question, did you have your glasses on that night?" She began to get a little flustered.

"No I did not have my glasses on but I know it was Mr. Jackson." "

Mrs. Morgan, thank you so much for your time." I stood up to leave and she walked me back through the house to the front door.

"What do you think will happen to Mr. Jackson? It is a shame what happened because he was always a nice neighbor."

"We will have to let the courts decide his fate. Once again, thank you." I left Mrs. Morgan's house feeling pretty good that I would be able to discredit this so-called eyewitness.

5

DISTRACTIONS

$\mathcal{I}$ drove home to meet with Danny. I made it home in time to take a trip before Danny arrived. My doorbell rang promptly at 4pm and I went to let him in.

"Hey Danny, come in and have a seat."

"Thanks Savannah." He walked into the living room and took a seat on the sofa. He looked nervous but I wanted to reassure him that there was no need to be nervous.

"Danny you can relax. I know that you came over to end our relationship and I am ok with that. My only hope is that we can continue to be friends." A wave of relief washed over his face.

"I am glad you understand and I would love to remain friends." My phone started ringing.

"Excuse me while I take his call." I went into the kitchen to answer the call.

"Hello."

"Savannah, you need to come to New York Presbyterian hospital as soon as possible. Your sister has been in a terrible accident." I could hear the panic in my mother's voice.

"I am on my way." I ran into the living room.

"Danny, my sister has been in a bad accident and I need to get to the hospital."

"You are visibly upset so I will take you to the hospital. What hospital is she in?"

"She is at New York Presbyterian." As we drove to the hospital, I was wondering how bad was her accident and would she even welcome me at her bedside. Regardless of how Nina felt, I love my sister. When we got to the hospital emergency, I went to look for my parents. I found them in the waiting room.

"Mom, what happened? Hi Dad!"

"Your sister was drinking and decided to drive. Her blood alcohol level was .13. She is having surgery but her spinal cord has been severed and she will be paralyzed from the waist down."

I was in total shock and all I could think about was taking a trip. I did not know what to say so I just sat down. My father sat next to me and hugged me as I cried.

"Pudding, can you help your sister from a legal

perspective? She will be facing DWI charges." My father always called me pudding.

"I will definitely help her. I will try to get her probation but she will probably also have to attend AA meetings. But the first priority is getting her through her medical ordeal. Are the doctors certain she will never walk again?"

"They said it is a very high probability. She will need to go to rehab before she can come home. We will get nurses to come in to help."

"Listen Dad, you and mom will not have to take this on by yourself. I want Nina to come and stay with me. I will help her through this." My father looked surprised.

"That is so nice of you but you know how you two get along; do you think that is a good idea?"

"There comes a time when you have to put your differences aside. I love my sister and I am going to do all that I can to help her. She will fight me but I am ready for the fight." Both my parents came in for a big hug.

"We love you and we are so proud of you."

I was not sure what I just got myself into but I felt It was my duty. Danny was still at the hospital with us.

"Danny, you don't have to stay. I will let you know how she is doing."

"I want to stay at least until she gets out of surgery. If that is ok with you?" Danny was a good friend and I was lucky to have him as my friend.

"Of course you can stay and thank you." The doctors

came to update us. Nina had been in surgery for 4 hours and she was now in ICU. It would be awhile before we would be able to see her. I let Danny take me home so I could drive my own car back to the hospital. I took a shower and took a trip. I called Bill to let him know what was going on.

"Hey Bill, I will definitely be able to discredit our star eyewitness. She is visually impaired and she did not have her glasses on when she claimed to see Dante. So things are looking better. I want to do some more digging on the girlfriend because I need to find out who would want to kill her and then shift the focus to that person. I won't be in the office for a while because my sister was in a bad car accident."

"Wow Savannah, I am sorry to hear that. Is she ok?"

"She is alive but she severed her spinal cord and she will probably never walk again. Once she is out of rehab, she will be staying with me."

"What do you need from me? Do you want me to reassign this case to someone else?" Bill had no intention of reassigning the case but he needed to say that to appear concerned.

"No Bill, I will be able to handle this case. I will have around the clock nurses to assist so other than my sister's hatred for me, I will be fine." Bill knew about the difficulties in our relationship and always believed that deep down Nina loved me.

"If you need anything, please let me know."

"Thanks Bill. I will talk to you later."

I went back to the hospital and my sister was able to have visitors. My parents were with her. I stood outside of her room contemplating what I would say to her. I did not want to upset her but I wanted her to know that I was there and I cared. I walked into the room and when she saw me, she just started crying. I went over to her bed and my mother moved out of the way. I bent over and kissed her forehead and whispered, "We will get through this together and I love you." She closed her eyes and the tears continued to roll down her face. We did not say anything after that and I just held her hand.

I spoke to Bill about my sister's case and he said he would take care of everything. He got Nina three years probation and mandatory AA meetings. Until she was able to attend meetings, a counselor would come to the house to meet with her. I got my house ready to receive Nina. I ordered the appropriate hospital bed, added bars in my shower and converted my guest room into a fitness room for her physical therapy. It would be 2 months before she could come home. In the meantime, I visited her daily and we never talked about our relationship until now.

"Savannah, I want to thank you for all that you are doing for me. I know that I have not been nice to you. I was mean to you because I was not happy with my own life. Instead of taking responsibility for my failures, I chose to lash out at you. You did not deserve any of the hatred that I threw at you. Please forgive me and I will try to do better."

"I forgive you and I love you. We are going to focus on you getting better."

"But I will never walk again so how much better will I get?"

"Getting better includes adjusting to your new life and finding ways to grow mentally instead of physically. There are so many successful people that are in wheelchairs because of paralysis but they found a way to live and be happy. Nina you have a lot to be thankful for and a long journey ahead of you but you won't have to do it alone. And I am not perfect Nina. I have my demons that I deal with also but I do a great job at covering them up." She looked at me and smiled. For the first time that I could remember, my sister and I were getting along.

6

WHO IS ELYSE?

I need to find out more about Elyse. I need to see if she had any enemies and if there is someone else that had a motive to murder her. Elyse's best friend from college was Maxine Graham. Maxine lives in Newark, New Jersey but works in lower Manhattan. I called her and scheduled to meet her during her lunch break. We met at Cafe Grumpy on the lower east side. When I arrived, Maxine was already there.

"Hi, you must be Maxine?" She reached out and we shook hands.

"Yes I am and nice to meet you. I was surprised that you wanted to meet me because Elyse and I have not spoken in a few years."

"I know that but I just wanted to know more about your relationship and why you did not stay in contact with one another." She looked a little agitated by my question.

"You know how some people just drift apart."

"My understanding was you and Elyse were very close friends. I am surprised that you did not stay in contact with one another. Was there a rift between the two of you?" She started looking around as if making sure we were not being watched.

"Listen, Elyse got involved with people that I was not comfortable with. That is the reason that we parted ways." I was starting to get somewhere with Maxine so I wanted to be careful how I proceeded.

"Can you tell me about these people?"

"Let's get something straight, I am not testifying and I will deny any and everything I tell you. These people play for keeps and I love being alive."

"Do you think that these people could be responsible for Elyse's death?"

"I don't know but it could be possible. There was a side of Elyse that no one knew about. She liked the bad girl persona and at time she would run with the wrong people. She started gambling and borrowing a lot of money from the wrong people. From my understanding she was over $500,000.00 in debt."

"But why didn't she get money from her father or Dante?"

"Because they would ask questions and discover her

gambling problem." This was not the type of information I was expecting to uncover.

"Is there any way you can point me in the right direction so I don't have to get you involved?"

"I know that she developed a friendship with Frank Morelli."

"Frank Morelli the mob boss?"

"You did not hear that from me. Look I have said more than I should have and I have to get back to work. Good luck." She left but I sat there for a few moments reviewing my notes and trying to decide how to move forward. I think I was going to pay a visit to Frank Morelli but first I need to stop by the office and talk to Bill.

When I got to the office Bill was in a meeting. I decided to do some research on Frank Morelli while I waited. Frank had his hands in a host of illegal activities; number running, drugs, human trafficking, murder and who know what else. He was never directly connected to any murders but most knew his hands were dirty. As I was doing my research, Bill popped his head in my office.

"What you got for me?" I motioned for him to come in.

"Looks like our Elyse was not the perfect little girl she would have had us to believe. She was a closet bad girl. Huge gambling debt and ties to Frank Morelli." I waited a few moments while Bill digested what I just told him.

"Wow I was not expecting that news. What's your next

move?" He sat back in his chair waiting for my answer. I felt like this was a test.

"I am going to pay a visit to Frank Morelli." He did not look surprised.

"I expected you to say that but I must caution you to be very careful because I do not want you to put yourself in danger. Just snoop around a little and don't push him. I am serious Savannah, be careful." Bill was right about being careful.

"I will also meet with Dante and see if he knew anything about his girlfriend's dark side." Bill stood up and looked directly at me.

"Let me repeat, I need you to be very careful with Frank Moretti, understand?"

"I understand." He left my office and I started to call Frank but decided I would just show up and request a meeting.

Frank Morelli owned a real estate company in Brooklyn. This was one of many businesses he used as a front for most of his illegal activities. I parked in front of the office. As I walked to the entrance, I was stopped by two men that looked like professional bodybuilders. The man to my right spoke first.

"Do you have an appointment?"

"No. I am attorney Savannah Taylor and I just needed a few minutes of Mr. Morelli's time."

"Let me see if he can see you." He walked into the office and returned quickly. "He will see you." I followed him into the office and Frank greeted me with a big smile.

"Hi Ms. Taylor. Please have a seat." I took a seat in front of his desk. "Now how can I be of service?" He was handsome and very charismatic.

"I represent Dante Jackson and I am following up on some leads."

"Yes, the boxer that killed his girlfriend."

"Allegedly killed his girlfriend." He winked at me.

"Well how can I help?"

"I have sources that tell me you and Elyse knew each other."

"Yes I knew Elyse very well." I was taken aback. I did not expect him to confess to knowing Elyse.

"What was the nature of your relationship with Elyse?" He looked at me with the devious smile.

"Elyse and I were not having an affair in case that was one of your thoughts. She was just a good friend and we hung out from time to time. When her boyfriend was out of town, she would get lonely and we would hang out and party. She did not want anyone to know about our friendship because most would make it out to be something sinister."

"Did you and Elyse ever argue? You do understand that I have to ask that question?" He chuckled and stood up.

"I never argued with Elyse and to answer your ultimate question, I would never hurt Elyse." I was not sure that I believed him but I could not see a motive and I did not want to risk pissing him off with further questioning.

"Thank you Mr. Morelli."

"Please call me Frank. You are welcome and please let me know if there is anything else I can assist you with." I left his office almost sure he was lying. I needed to dig a little deeper to see if I could come up with another suspect to shift focus to. I went back to my office and started digging into Elyse's friends. I made a list and started calling some of her friends.

Most gave me the same "she was a good girl" line but somehow I felt like they all knew more than they were telling me. The last one on my list was Celeste Wingate. They grew up together and remained friends.

"Hi, can I speak with Celeste?"

"Who is speaking?" "My name is Savannah Taylor and…" she cut me off before I could finish.

"Yeah, I know who you are. What can I do for you?" She did not seem like she wanted to talk with me.

"I wanted to know if you could talk to me about Elyse? I am trying to get to know who she was and who would have been responsible for killing her."

"I am not going to tell you anything, except you have the wrong person. Dante would have never hurt Elyse. And Elyse was not the good girl everyone would have you to believe. Sometimes I wondered why Dante put up with her. Listen, I have to go and there is nothing more I have to say." She hung up the phone and I was left with more questions and no answers. She made it a sound like Dante might have known about Elyse's dark side. I was not sure which direction to go but I decided to call it quits and go and check on Nina.

When I got home, Nina was asleep. The accident truly changed her. She was my loving sister. We were able to have a conversation without arguing. I just stood in the doorway staring at her and wished I could make everything alright for her. I hated seeing her suffer.

"Don't just stand there staring at me. Come sit with me." Nina used her remote control to raise her bed so she was in an upright position.

"I did not mean to wake you up." She smiled at me.

"I was not really sleep. I just had my eyes closed. What's going on with you Savannah?" I was not sure what she was asking. Even though she had changed, I still had my guard up.

"What do you mean? You know I'm just working hard on this case. It is one of the biggest cases of my career." Nina was looking at me as though she was looking directly into my soul.

"Savannah I am not talking about work. I just want to know are you happy? I don't want to see work replace your happiness. I love you and I want only the best for you." I was not used to this Nina and for some reason it unnerved me. No one has ever tried to dig into my feelings and I am not sure that I was comfortable.

"Nina I love you too, but please don't worry about me because I am fine. Your focus needs to be on your well-being and you getting better. How is your therapy going?"

Nina chuckled, "Nice way to get the focus off yourself. I will leave it alone for now, but I want you to know I sincerely want you to be happy. Therapy is going well but sometimes I wonder why am I doing this if I'm never gonna walk again. I have no feeling and I just don't know what good therapy is actually doing."

Suddenly I had a thought, "What do you think about you helping me on this case? It would give you something to do and I sure could use the help." She looked at me with a puzzled look on her face.

"How am I supposed to help you on your case? Did you forget that I am paralyzed?"

"Of course not, but you are paralyzed from the waist down. I can use another set of eyes and another perspective when reviewing this case. I will get you a laptop and you can do research for me. I think this time together and working together would be fun. What do you say?" She thought about it for a few seconds.

"What the heck, count me in!"

Tomorrow when you get your laptop, I will send you all the information on the case and you can review it and let me know your thoughts. In the meantime, you get some rest and I am going to get some. I stood up and kissed her forehead.

"When you are ready I am here." For some reason I

think there was another meaning to what she said but I left it alone because I needed to take a trip.

I needed to focus on preparing my opening statement for the trial. First I would work on discrediting the eyewitness. That would be an easy task. Next I would have to paint a different picture of Elyse. But I need to come up with another person to focus on as the murderer. And that was where I was stuck. I went out to Best Buy and picked up a computer for Nina and decided to stay home and work on this case.

7

PUTTING THE PIECES TOGETHER

*N*ina enjoyed working with me and I was also enjoying my sister.

"Hey Savannah, do you really believe the mob boss is the real murderer?" I really did not think Frank Morelli killed Elyse.

"Nina I am not sure but I need someone to put the focus on and I need that person quick." Nina was in deep thought. "Nina, do you have a thought?"

"Something about Elyse's behavior just is not adding up. I mean it was like living a double life. Most of the time someone who lives a double life is running from something. Now if we believe that she and Dante are so happy, then what else could she be running from?" Everything that Nina said is true but I am still left with a mystery person. I need to learn more about Elyse.

"I think you should interview her friend again. The

one who told you about Frank Morelli and also talk to Dante again. If they were as close as he said he has to know some of the people that put her on edge." Wow, Nina was getting the hang of this real quick.

"Alright Attorney Nina, I will re-interview her friend and I will talk to Dante. We make a great team, don't you think?"

Nina eyes teared up and she smiled at me. "I am so sorry for the way I have treated you all these years. This has been a very humbling experience and I want to make it up to you." I sat on the edge of her bed and took her hand.

"You don't have to make anything up to me. Let's just take advantage of this fresh start." Her face brightened up.

"I have actually given some thought to taking an online course to become a paralegal. What do you think?"

"I think you would be excellent and why stop there, you could be a great attorney." We both bust out laughing.

I decided to call Maxine and see if I could set up a second meeting with her. I called her number and got no answer. I left a voicemail but I was not expecting a return phone call. To my surprise she did call me back.

"Maxine, thank you for returning my call. I was wondering if we could meet again?" There was a hesitation before she answered.

"I am not sure. Look I really hope you get the right

person responsible for Elyse's murder, but I am not sure how you think I could help. I told you all that I know."

"Ok, instead of meeting, can you tell me if there was anyone else that Elyse did not get along with and please take your time?" There was a brief pause.

"The only other person I can think of is her dad." This came as a surprise because I got the picture that they had a perfect relationship.

"What do you mean her dad? I was under the impression that Elyse and her father had a good relationship. What makes you say that?"

"I really don't know details but there were times where she was frustrated with her father." There was nothing much here.

"Thanks for your help Maxine."

What daughters do not get frustrated with their father at times. Maybe I will pay her father a visit, but right now I need to prepare my opening statement because the trial was scheduled to begin next week. I checked my phone and there was a voicemail. I played it and to my surprise it was Jeffrey.

"Hey Savannah, this is Jeffrey. I just thought you might want some information regarding your case. I am not trying to harass you but I have some information that might be important. Give me a call when you get a chance." I did not know how to react and I wonder what he was up to; I find it very hard to trust Jeffrey. But my curiosity was getting the best of me. I decided a phone call could not hurt. I dialed his number and it rang 4 times and I was prepared to hang up, when he picked.

"Hello,"

I hesitated before answering. "Hi Jeffrey, this is Savannah. I am returning your call."

"Listen Savannah, I just want to clear the air before I continue. I apologize for my remark at the courtroom. I just want you to know, I wish you no harm. I have been in counseling for a while and also AA meetings. I wanted you to know this before I continued. I came across some information that you might want to follow up on. Dante and Elyse have a mutual friend in the Las Vegas area. He is doing a lot of talking about the murder. Not sure what it will produce, but thought you might want the information. When we hang up, I will text the information to you." This might be worth checking out.

"I will check it out. I might even fly out to Vegas. I know he has a lot of matches out there so maybe I can speak to some folks while there."

"I will try to get you some names if you decide to go to Vegas." I was taken aback by the new Jeffrey but I still was cautious.

"Jeffrey, thank you for the things you said and I wish you nothing but the best. Also thank you for all of your help with this case. I appreciate all of it."

"You are welcome and good luck. I will talk with you later."

"Ok, bye." I waited for Jeffrey to text the information to me. The name he texted me was Derrick Wilkins.

I went to check on Nina and she was wide awake working on her computer.

"Aren't you the busy bee? How are you doing?" She put her laptop aside.

"I am feeling better than I have in a while or should I say, since the accident. Thank you for giving me purpose again. It has been hard to deal with knowing I will be wheelchair bound. I have a different outlook on life now thanks to you." I was speechless and thankful that I had my sister.

"What are you working on?"

"Just reviewing all the notes but something just doesn't add up. I don't think our mob boss is the right guy. I made a few phone calls to some contacts of mine and rumors are our mob boss really admired Elyse. He was more like a father figure. I also heard that he has a bounty out for anyone with information that leads to the murderer. He does not believe that it is Dante either." I was blown away at all this information that Nina has put together.

"Wow, you are amazing at this and I did not have unsavory contacts." We both bust out in a laugh.

"Yes I have to agree with you, I don't think mob boss is the answer. I have a lead that Jeffrey gave me and..."

"Wait a minute! Hold up! Jeffrey?"

"Yes you heard me right. I think he has changed but I

am being very cautious when dealing with him." Nina gave me a stern look but softened it with a smile.

"I don't want to see you get hurt. I trust your judgement but please be careful." I knew she had my best interest at heart.

"I will be very careful. Will you be ok if I go to Vegas for a couple of days?"

"I will be fine. Delores will take good care of me."

Delores was her nurse's aide and she has been great.

"I have a little research to do and I also have to meet with Bill to update him. It will only be for a couple of days. I want to get out there and back before the trial starts." I cleared everything with Bill and got some more names of people to check out from Jeffrey. I booked my flight and set up some appointments. My flight was at 6 am in the morning. I was leaving from JFK so I needed to get to the airport by 4 am. JFK is a mad house on Tuesday mornings. I made sure that everything Nina needed was in place. Delores was a life saver. I packed my bags, went in to say good night to Nina and went in my room to take a trip.

I arrived at the airport at 3:45 am and just as I thought, it was a madhouse. I only had a carry on, so I headed straight to security. As I stood in line the lady in front of me turned around.

"Hey aren't you the lawyer that is representing that boxer?" This happens when you are handling a high profile case.

"Yes I am." she turned all the way around prepared to start a conversation. "I am not allow to discuss the case." She was determined to slip a question in.

"Do you think he did it?"

"Like I said, I can't discuss the case." She smirked at me and turned back around.

It took me 25 minutes to get through security. I got to my gate at 5:05. I got a cup of coffee and sat and read the newspaper. The plane was scheduled to board at 5:35 so this left me 30 mins to relax. This was going to be slightly difficult for me because I could not bring any drugs with me because of airport security. Last thing I needed was getting busted at the airport with drugs. Career will be over. I will take a drink at times to take the edge off. I took a look at my notes and my first appointment was with Derrick Wilkins. I also had an appointment scheduled with the boxing promoter, Tito Sanchez, this afternoon. My phone started ringing and it was Jeffrey. I did not want this to get personal with him. I wanted to keep this a business relationship for now. I answered the phone.

"Hey Jeffrey, I am at the airport. What did you need?" I wanted to get straight to the point.

"That's a loaded question. I just wanted to let you know of someone else that you might want to see while you are there. Elyse's aunt lives in Vegas. It can't hurt to pay her a visit." I felt bad because he was calling about business.

"Thank you for that information." There was a slight pause.

"Listen Savannah, I know that you can't trust me right now and I truly understand. I am not asking for anything right now. What I am hoping for in the future is a friendship. Nothing intimate, just friends. I am willing to wait and I will definitely respect the boundaries. Have a safe trip and good luck." I started to hang up.

"Wait a minute Jeffrey. You hurt me and it will take time for me to trust your friendship. I appreciate your help and I am proud of you for taking the necessary steps to get help. Let's take baby steps and see where that takes us as friends. Is that ok with you?"

"Of course it is and thank you. I will talk to you later." I hung up and was not sure what just transpired. I was still hesitant but I was willing to give him a chance. It was time to get on the plane. I was flying JetBlue and I upgraded to the extra leg room. It was a straight through flight. As soon as we were in the air, I asked for a Jack and Coke. I had three of those and I slept the whole flight. When the flight landed in Vegas, I got a taxi and headed to the hotel. I called and checked on Nina.

"Hey sis, just checking on you. Are you ok?" She was laughing.

"Mom and Dad have called also every hour on the hour and now you. I am fine and Delores will keep me in check. But make sure that you call me after your meetings to tell me what you find out."

"I will and love you!"

I booked a room at Aria and check-in was a breeze. I called room service and requested a bottle of Jack. Next on the agenda was a nice hot shower. It was noon and my first meeting was at 3 pm. So I pulled out my laptop and poured a glass of Jack. I was scheduled to meet Derek at Ferraro's Italian restaurant. I got to the restaurant at 2:45 and got a table. Derek arrived about 10 minutes later.

"Miss Taylor?"

"Yes and please call me Savannah. May I call you Derek?"

"Of course." He sat down. He was not what I expected. He was about 6'2 and he had a mocha complexion. He was very handsome.

"Thank you for taking time to talk with me. Would you like something to eat or drink?"

"I will take a beer but nothing to eat." I called the waiter over and ordered a beer and some cheese and nachos.

"How is Dante holding up?"

"He is doing alright under the circumstances. So how do you know Dante and Elyse?"

"I went to school with Elyse and when she started dating Dante, we all became friends. Dante seemed alright and I never had any problems with him. I do believe he really loved Elyse but sometimes he just seemed strange and I just can't put my finger on it." This was not going in the direction I expected.

"What do you mean by strange?" He pondered the questions for a few seconds.

"It seemed that sometimes he would get in a sad mood and then disappear. It was like he just wanted to be alone. I guess there is nothing wrong with that. I just found it strange at times. I will tell you the best person to speak would be Elyse's Aunt Naomi. That woman treats me just like I am family and I love her to death. Later on I would see Dante more than Elyse because he had a lot of fights in Vegas. He would always get tickets for me. Once again he would disappear to be alone at times. I just blamed it on boxing." Not sure that meant anything much but I wrote it down in my notes.

"Do you have a phone number and address for Ms. Naomi?"

"She lives in the Onyx Apartments and the address is 5150 Duke Ellington Way. I will text you her phone number, just give me your phone number." He flashed the sexiest smile. I can't believe he is trying to flirt with me. As tempting as he might be, I was not interested at the moment.

"How about you just write it down for me?" He chuckled.

"Shot down but I tried. It is not often I meet a beautiful, smart and successful woman and let her get away without at least one date." Real smooth but I was not convinced.

"You can count this as your one date." He stood up to leave and he took my hand and kissed it.

"It has been a pleasure, and next you are in Vegas, let me take you on a real date." Very charming and I was almost tempted.

"I will keep that invite in mind. Thank you for meeting with me."

After he left I called Ms. Naomi and she was more than willing to talk to me. I called Tito Sanchez to see if I could reschedule our appointment for tomorrow. That worked out fine. I was on my way to Naomi's apartment and I wonder if this trip was even worth it. I tried to stay optimistic but not sure what I was looking for. I got to Noami a little after 4 pm. Before I could ring her bell, she was opening the door.

"You must be Savannah. You don't mind me calling you Savannah?" I stepped into her apartment.

"Not at all. Wow, you have a beautiful home Ms. Naomi." She showed me into the living room.

"Please have a seat and tell me how I can help you. I don't want to see Dante pay for a crime he did not commit." I decided to try a different approach.

"Can you think of anyone that would want to kill Elyse?"

"I really can't think of anyone but if I had to choose someone other than Dante, it would be her dad." I could not believe what I just heard.

"Excuse me, did you say her dad?"

"Yes, I said her dad. I want to believe things have changed but I need to tell you about Elyse and her father's past. It might not have any bearing on this case but I believe you need to know. Elyse's mother died during childbirth. Now my brother loved Eleanor to death. Eleanor was Elyse's mother. It is beautiful when a husband loves and honors his wife, but my brother's love for his wife was almost psychotic. If he was out of his wife's presence for any length of time he was miserable. I told him one time that it was unhealthy to love someone the way he loved Eleanor. I don't know why I said that because he put me out of his house and did not speak to me for more than a month. When Eleanor got pregnant I thought that this would be good for Robert. Someone else for him to project his love towards. Eleanor had a complicated pregnancy and she was put on bed rest when she was seven months. Robert waited on his wife hand and foot. Now don't get me wrong, he was a good husband and they had a great marriage. Eleanor carried Elyse full term but when she went into labor, she started hemorrhaging. She also had developed eclampsia which led to seizures. She died 6 hours after giving birth. Robert was inconsolable and he refused to hold or look as his new baby girl. At the hospital I tried to comfort him and convince him to see his baby girl. He looked me in my eyes and said,

"If it wasn't for her my wife would still be alive!" It was a horrible situation.

I brought Elyse home to stay with me. I thought that after the funeral and a short grieving process, Robert would want to see his daughter. Elyse stayed with me until she was 10 years old. I raised her as my own and it was hard to let her go when Robert finally decided he wanted to be a father. Many times Elyse would call me and say she wanted to come home. I would ask her if her father treating her ok and she would always say, I am alright, I just want to come home. As time went on she had finally adjusted. They were never as close as he wanted people to believe." I was not expecting this.

"But do you think he would be capable of killing his daughter?" She hesitated for a quick second.

"Yes, I believe he is capable. I have bad feelings in my heart. I love my brother but he is not right in the head. Dante does not deserve to suffer if he is innocent." I closed my notebook that I was using to take notes.

"Ms. Naomi, you have been helpful. Is there anything else you can think of that might be of importance?" She looked at me with a devilish smile.

"Nothing else, but you have made quite the impression on Derrick." I started blushing.

"Did he call you?"

"Yes he did. He has asked for my help with convincing you to have dinner with him tomorrow night." Wow, this guy was very persistent. Well dinner couldn't hurt, besides I will be leaving Vegas and him behind.

"Tell him to call me at my hotel and we can arrange a

dinner date. I can't believe you tricked me into this." We both laughed and she gave me a hug.

"Thank you for helping with this case. Elyse was like a daughter to me and I want the person responsible to pay.

When I got back to the hotel there was a message for me, and I was not surprised that it was Derrick. I did not call him back right away. Instead I took a nice hot shower. I got out my laptop and poured myself a glass of Jack. I was a little edgy but nothing I could not handle. For the very first time, I thought about getting help for my addition. Part of the reason I keep men at a distance is my addiction. I didn't want a man snooping around and finding my dirty little secret. But I would have to wait until after the trial was over. I picked up my phone to call Derek and he answered on the first ring.

"Hi Derek?"

"Yes Savannah. How are you doing?" He even sounded sexy over the phone.

"I was told you had a pending dinner date in the works." He could not help but laugh.

"Yes if you would do me the honor and join me tomorrow night for dinner, that would make my day." I realized that I was smiling from ear to ear.

"Yes I would love to and what time should I be ready?"

"I will pick you at your hotel at 5 pm if that is ok?"

"That works well for me. See you then."

As I hung up the phone I could not help but notice

that I was excited about going out on a date. I had not felt this way in such a long time. I needed to check on Nina. When I dial the number, the phone rang five times. Just as I was about to panic, she picked up the phone.

"Hey Nina, did I wake you up."

"I was reading a book and dozed off. How are things going?" I was glad to have someone to talk to.

"Odd turn of events. I went to visit Elyse's aunt and she told me that when Elyse was born, her father resented her because her mother died in childbirth. She actually brought Elyse home from the hospital and she stayed with her aunt until she was 10 years old. I think the aunt believes the father could be capable of murder. I planned to interview him again once I return. I think I will take Jeffrey with me, if he agrees, just in case. On another note, guess who has a date tonight?" Nina squealed with delight.

"What the hell are you doing in Vegas? Tell me everything."

"Well, the date is with Derrick Wilkins."

"The guy you went there to interview?" I could imagine what Nina was thinking.

"I know it sounds crazy but he was so persistent on taking me out. Went as far as calling Elyse aunt for assistance. But do not worry, I will be careful and it is just a simple date. I am not looking for anything more. But damn, he is so fine!" We both busted out laughing.

"Savannah do you think the father is a possible murder?" I thought about it carefully.

"The man I met does not seem cable of murder but then again some people have mastered the art of deception. I will look into it further when I get home."

"Ok, call me tomorrow and let me know how your other interviews and date go."

For the rest of the evening, I drank Jack and watched tv. I was watching a program called Cold Case Files and they were talking about an unknown serial killer that seems to attack in spurts and the murders have gone cold. All of his victims were strangled and he has killed seven women to date. I love watching this show. While they went to a commercial break and I got up and poured myself another glass of Jack. I was back in front of the tv as they continued talking about the serial killer. The report talks about the similarities in the murders. All the women had a small x carved into their shoulder with a knife. I could not believe what I was hearing. Could this be a coincidence? It can't be because Dante lives cross country. But what are the chances that this serial killer is killing his victims the same way Dante attacked those women he told me about. I called Nina immediately.

"Hey Nina, I need you to do some research for me. I am going to send you 7 dates and I need you to find out if Dante was in Vegas at these times."

"What's going?" I did not want to give her all the details until I knew what I was dealing with.

"I am just checking a lead. When I know more I will fill you in and get that info to me as soon as you are done." I hung up and sat there thinking to myself, what are the chances that I am defending a serial killer.

It was hard for me to sleep because my mind was racing. Do I put this out of my mind and focus on the case at hand? I decided to continue representing Dante but I still needed to check further into these murders. I was finally able to get a little sleep.

I met the promoter, Tito Sanchez, at a little coffee shop inside of my hotel. He had a very thick accent but I was able to understand what he was saying.

"Tito, do you know if Dante had any enemies that may have killed his wife as a way to get his attention?" Tito did not take a moment to think. His answer was quick.

"Dante did not have any enemies that I knew about. He was a good guy."

"Do you know if he saw other women when he was in town without his wife?" He frowned as if I said something wrong.

"Dante never talked to or looked at other women. He loved his wife." Tito was definitely a Dante fan.

"Tito thanks for taking time to talk with me. If you think of anything that might be significant, please call me." I handed him my business card. I cancelled the rest of my appointments. I needed some down time before my date tonight with Derrick. I was almost tempted to cancel but I need to take my mind off this case for a little while.

Derrick was taking me to Top of the World, the restaurant is on the 106th floor of the Stratosphere Tower. His choice was impressive. I decided to wear this black cocktail dress that I brought with me. It highlighted all of my curves. I wore a pair of Christian Louboutin red bottom black pumps. I put on a simple strain of pearls with matching earrings. I was ready for a relaxing night out on the town. He arrived promptly at 5pm. When I opened the door he was almost speechless.

"Wow! You look amazing and so beautiful!" I smiled and grabbed my shawl.

"Thank you and I must say you clean up very well yourself. You look very handsome tonight."

"Thank you ma'am." We got to the restaurant and we sat by the window; the view was breathtaking.

"Derrick, this view is awesome. I have always wanted to come here." The waiter came over to ask us what we wanted to drink. I ordered a glass of Cabernet Sauvignon since I planned on ordering the prime rib. We ate dinner and there was some small talk.

"Savannah, I am glad that you came out tonight. I was hoping that we could keep in touch. I know you live in New York but I just enjoy your company." As much as I was enjoying myself, there was no room in my life for a long distance relationship.

"Derrick, I am having a wonderful time but honestly, I can't promise anything. My life is complicated right now and I don't want to lead you on." He smiled graciously.

"I understand but you can't blame me for trying and I appreciate your honesty." My phone rang and it was Jeffrey. I silenced my phone and let the call go to voicemail.

"Did you need to take that call?" Derrick didn't miss a beat.

"No, it was work related so it could wait since I am not working right now. Derrick I want to run something by you. How close are you with Dante?"

"I would not say we are close, we became friends by default." I need to better understand their relationship.

"I understand you met him through Elyse but did you guys hang out outside of Elyse?" He thought about my question for a minute.

"Honestly we never hung out. And if I am honest, he was just a way for me to get ringside seats for his fights. As long as Elyse was happy. Why do you ask?" I did not know if I could trust Derrick but I wanted to see if he noticed anything that would put Dante at the scene of the murders.

"Well there have been a series of murders and they all happened on the same nights that Dante had a scheduled fight. Just trying to see if there is any connection." He chuckled.

"Aren't you trying to free Dante not get him convicted of multiple murders." Did I make a mistake by telling Derrick?

"No, I am committed to representing him but I can't

overlook something that seems to implicate him. I am not pursuing this, it just seemed to be very coincidental."

"You don't have to explain because if it was me, I would feel obligated. Let me know if I can help in any way."

"Thanks just wanted to see if you knew something about Dante that I didn't." Derrick escorted me back to my hotel after dinner.

"How about a nightcap?" I really wanted to say yes but I was scared what might happen.

"Not tonight Derrick. I have an early flight and I am tired. I enjoyed our date." He pulled out a business card. "Here is my card with my contact information. Use it anytime." I took the card and he leaned in for a kiss. I did not stop him and on top of being fine, he was a hell of a kisser.

8

THE GIG IS UP

J jumped into the shower and then poured myself a glass of Jack. I picked up my phone and called Jeffrey. He picked up on the second ring.

"Hello."

"Hey Jeffrey. I see you called earlier. What's up?" There was a slight hesitation.

"I was just checking to see how the interviews were going?" I could tell from Jeffrey's tone that he just wanted to talk to me.

"Well, I think I will need your help when I get home. I want to interview Elyse's father again but I will need you to go with me"

"Why, what's going on?" "I interviewed Mr. Daniels' sister and it seems that he resented his daughter when she was born. His daughter lived with her aunt until she was

10 years old and he did not want anything to do with her. He blamed her for the death of his wife. Not sure it means anything but I want to shake that tree and see what fruit falls."

"No problem, I will go with you. When you are coming back?" Jeffrey was so easy to talk to when he was not acting like a jerk. The counseling seems to be working for him. But I will proceed with caution.

"My flight leaves in the morning. I will call you when I get in." There was an awkward silence.

"Do you need someone to pick you up from the airport?"

"I was going to call an Uber but if you are offering, then I accept."

"I will see you tomorrow. Savannah, thank you." I was not sure why he was thanking me but I did not ask why. I was a little edgy but I decided it was time for me to think about quitting. I think after this case is over, I would check myself into a rehab facility. I decide to sit down with Nina and talk to her about my addiction. I felt like I could trust her and I really needed someone to talk to. I think Jeffrey has provided some motivation. If he could admit to his shortcomings and seek out help, then I would too. I put the Jack up and went to sleep. I had a terrible night's sleep. Withdrawal was starting and I was sick most of the night. About 2 in the morning, I jumped in the shower and tried to get myself together. I had some opioids as a backup. I popped two pills to help take the edge off. By the time I left for the airport, I started to feel better. When I got to the airport, I popped 2 more pills. While on the plane, I had 2 shots of Jack. I was not thinking about the deadly mixture of alcohol and pills. I just wanted to feel better. When we landed at JFK, my head was swimming. As I walked through the airport to the terminal exit, I felt like I was going to pass out. When I got to the exit door, I saw Jeffrey's car. He got out of the car to greet me and all of a sudden my head started spinning and the ground came up to meet my face. Next thing I remember is waking up in Jamaica hospital emergency room. My head felt heavy and I was so groggy. Jeffrey was sitting by my side.

"Hey Jeffrey, what happened?" He had a serious look of concern.

"You passed out. Savannah, talk to me. What is going on with you? I know there was a time where you could not trust me but I promise you I am not that man anymore. I care about you and always will. I can help you but I need you to trust me." Trust him? What the hell did he know?

"What are you talking about? I just got a little sick." He did not look convinced.

"Savannah, they found opioids and alcohol in your system. You could have died." All I could think was, the gig is up Savannah.

"I don't know what to say, other than I am destroyed."

"First off, I brought you here because I have a friend who owes me a few favors. So as far as anyone else is concerned, you were never here but we have to address the problem at hand." I decided to come clean. I need to talk to someone and I hope I was not making a mistake by putting my trust in Jeffrey.

"I am an addict. I was managing my addition and thought if I was not hurting anyone then what the hell. I got real sick in Vegas and that's why I am here now."

"You start going through withdrawal. Do you want to quit?"

"I thought I didn't but this weekend in Vegas, I made up my mind that I was going to quit after I finish this case." He looked at me like I was crazy.

"Savannah, you need to quit now. This case is not more important than your well being." There was no way that I was going to walk away from this case.

"Listen Jeffrey, I know that you will not understand but I will not walk away from this case and I need you to support me on this." He looked so torn but he was prepared to do anything to get back in my good graces.

"Listen I can talk to my doctor friend and see if we could put you on a methadone program until this case is over. After that I really want you to check into a rehab center. I will be there every step of the way. Please let me help you." I never imagine myself in this situation and needing help from Jeffrey.

"Jeffrey I am trusting you with my life, please don't let me down."

"Savannah, I had to learn the hard way the alcohol was my demon. I lost a lot because of my drinking, you included. I know what it is like to be addicted and I will never go down that road again. I am a totally different person when I drink. I am thankful for the counseling and the AA meetings. I have an accountability partner who keeps me focused and I am now mentoring young adults. You can do this but it will get hard before it gets easy. For now get some rest. Are you hungry?" The thought of food made my stomach turn. The doctor came in and gave me a lecture on how I am slowly killing myself. So I was put on Methadone to take the edge off. Jeffrey was driving me home. I was released from the hospital around 4pm and I realized I never called Nina and she must be worried. I dial her number and she picks up on the first ring. "Where have you been, Savannah? I was worried about you." I interrupted her.

"Nina, I am fine. I have a lot to tell you. I am on my way home. See you shortly."

When I got home, Jeffrey walked me to the door. "I will call you later." I did not want him to leave.

"Hey Jeffrey, will you come in while I talk to Nina?"

"Are you sure you want me to be there?" I did not have to think about it because I needed him at this moment.

"Yes I want you to be there." We went straight to Nina's room. She had a puzzled look on her face.

"Please don't tell me you two eloped!!" We could not help but laugh.

"No we did not elope." She did not let me finish. "I know this has something to do with your problem you have and I hope you are going to help her, not hurt her. Don't look at me that way, I knew you had a drug addiction but I was waiting for you to come and talk to me. I can understand not coming to me before my accident but now it is different. I care about you and I want the best for you." I was speechless because I never thought that she knew.

"How long have you known? I guess that doesn't matter. I am on a methadone program until this case is over and then I am going to check into a rehab facility. I just need both you to be there for me." Nina looked at Jeffrey with squinting eyes.

"Listen Jeffrey, I will not stand by and let my sister be hurt. You better do her right." I quickly jumped in.

"We are not dating, we are just friends." She looked at me with doubting eyes.

"Whatever, I am just putting him on notice. Both of you pull up a chair and tell me where you are with this case." I told her about my meeting with the aunt and Jeffrey and I were going to interview the father again tomorrow.

"Wow that is interesting, but do you think he could be a suspect?"

"I am not sure but I am going to check into it. We sat

up for another 2 hours just talking and enjoying each other's company. Jeffrey stood up to leave.

"Ladies, although I am enjoying your company, I have to leave. Savannah, what time do you want to pay a visit to Mr. Daniels?"

"I will give him a call in the morning to confirm a time and I will let you know if that is ok? I will walk you to the door." He bent over and gave Nina a kiss on the forehead.

"You take care of yourself Ms. Nina." She smiled at him as we left the room. When we got to the front door, he held my hand.

"Thank you for letting me be there for you today. I am going to help you through this and you come through this fine." I leaned in and kissed him on the check.

"Thank you and get home safely." I was developing a new found respect for Jeffrey and I like the new Jeffrey. I was on my way to my room to get ready for bed.

"Savannah stop in here please." I expected this was coming. I went into Nina's room and pulled up a chair beside her bed.

"Savannah, I love you and I think you made a big step today by deciding to get help. I will be here for you every step of the way. Also, I must say I enjoyed Jeffrey's company tonight. I like the new Jeffrey. But please take it slow. I don't want to see you hurt. I am glad he was there for you today. "

"Thank you Nina and I love you!" I was getting up to leave when she stopped me.

"I almost forgot; I checked those dates and Dante was in Vegas all of those times." What or who was I really dealing with?

9

THE BREAKDOWN

I woke up extra groggy because I had to take some methadone last night before I went to sleep. I hopped in the shower hoping that would make me feel better. It was 10 AM so I decided to call Mr. Daniels. The phone rang twice and then he picked up.

"Mr. Daniel, this is Savannah Taylor, and I wanted to know if I can meet with you this afternoon?" He hesitated for a moment.

"Is there something you found out regarding my daughter's murder?" I wanted to be careful how I answered this question because I didn't want to spook him.

"I just wanted to review what I found out so far and just asked you a few more questions. Do you have some time this afternoon?"

"Sure I will be available around 3 PM."

"Okay I will see you then, thank you."

After I hung up I dialed Jeffrey's number to let them know what time we were going to meet with Mr. Daniels.

"Hello." He actually sounded as if he just woke up.

"Did I wake you?"

"No you did not wake me, I was just relaxing."

"Mr. Daniels will see us today at 3 PM." It was strange but I was actually sitting here thinking about what Jeffrey had on right now.

"Did you tell him that I was coming with you?"

"No I didn't; but we will cross that bridge when we get there."

He hesitated for a moment like he wanted to say something else but instead he just said, "see you later."

I decided to spend time around the house and keep Nina company until it was time for our meeting with Mr. Daniels.

"Savannah have you given any thought about talking to Bill. If you are going away to rehab, you have to tell him. I think you have a good enough relationship with him and he would understand."

"You are right, I will eventually have to talk to him. I believe Bill will understand, but I am still so embarrassed to talk about this to anyone outside of you and Jeffrey."

"Your first priority has to be getting better and that is all that counts." We spent the rest of the morning and early afternoon talking. Around 1 pm I went and got dressed. Just as I was putting on my shoes, the doorbell rang. I opened the door and it was Jeffrey.

"Are you ready, pretty lady?" I was loving the flattery.

"Yes, just let me grab my purse."

When we arrived at Mr. Daniels place, Jeffrey turned off the engine but did not move to get out of the car.

"Savannah, I need to tell you something before we get out of the car. I love you and I am not looking for anything from you. I just needed to tell you that. Now let's go question Mr. Daniels." I was not expecting that and I did not know how to respond.

"Jeffrey, we will talk about this later."

We walked to Mr. Daniels and rang his doorbell.

"Hi Miss Taylor, I see you brought someone with you." We step into his apartment.

"This is Jeffrey Johnston and he is also working with me on this case." I purposely left out that Jeffrey was a detective.

"Have a seat, can I get either of you something to drink?" We both declined.

"Mr. Daniels, can you tell me a little more about Elyse's childhood?" Mr. Daniel sat down in the recliner that was facing the couch that Jeffrey and I were sitting on.

"Well, she is like most little girls. Nothing that stands out."

"Isn't it true that you did not take custody of your daughter until she was 10 years old?"

"It was her fault and it took me some time to get over that." Mr. Daniel had a glazed look in his eyes, like he just left this planet.

"What was her fault?"

"I loved Eleanor and she died. It was her fault." It was like he was becoming detached with reality.

"Mr. Daniels, who are you talking about when you say, it was her fault?" Jeffrey and I looked at each other.

"I tried to forgive her but I was told that she had to pay for her sins."

"Who told you that?" He stood up and started pacing the floor.

"She could not take Eleanor from me without paying. I had to wait a long time before I could make her pay."

"Mr. Daniels, how did you make her pay?"

"I tried to love her but I could not because she took my Eleanor. Eleanor was my whole world." Jeffrey and I both knew what we were dealing with and we needed to proceed with caution. I let Jeffrey take over.

"Mr. Daniels, I know how it is when you are robbed of the love of your life. Let us help you make her pay."

"It's too late, I took care of everything." Jeffrey slowly approached Mr. Daniel with his handcuffs in his hand. Mr. Daniels did not resist as Jeffrey put on the handcuffs and then miranderized him.

"Mr. Daniels, do you want to tell me what happened to your daughter or do you want a lawyer?" He looked up at me with tears in his eyes.

"I had to send her to Eleanor. Only Eleanor could forgive her." I could already envision an insanity plea. We took him down to police headquarters, where they offered him a public defender but he wanted to confess. There was a part of me that felt sorry for him.

"So I guess you will visit Dante and deliver the good news."

"Yeah I guess I will but I need to talk something over with you. Do you have time for lunch?" He looked at his phone.

"I am free for now. I know a quaint little pizza spot just a couple of blocks from here." I knew I should call Bill but I needed to talk to Jeffrey first about what I discovered while in Vegas. As soon as we got to the pizza shop Jeffrey ordered 2 slices of cheese and pepperoni.

"Do you want a couple of slices?"

"No, I will just have a Pepsi." We found a table in the back.

"So what's up?"

"Well, while I was in Vegas I was watching this cold case tv show. They were highlighting a series of murders in the Vegas area. They were the work of a serial killer. Well something caught my attention about these cases. All the women who were murder had a X carved into their shoulders."

"Ok, so what does that mean?"

"Well, Dante had some issues in his past with some women. He choked them out and carved an X into their shoulder. I had Nina check all the dates of the murders to see if Dante was in Vegas and he was there on every date. I know he is my client but I feel like I need to investigate further."

"Wait a minute Savannah. I get where you are coming from but you are not a detective and if it turns out that Dante is a serial killer, you are putting yourself in danger by trying to pursue this."

"Well, will you help me? It is just so coincidental. I believe he is the serial killer." Jeffrey sat up in his chair and leaned in to talk to Savannah. "Listen I will help you but you need to leave the investigation stuff to me. Because if this is true, then Dante is very dangerous." I agreed to let Jeffrey do the investigation.

"Well I need to go into the office and talk to Bill and then have Dante processed out of jail. Can you drop me off at home so I can get my car?"

"Of course and remember what I told you, leave the snooping around to me." I smiled at him.

"I promise I will leave it to you."

When I got to the office, I went straight to Bill's office. I knocked on his door.

"Come in!"

"Hey Bill, I have some good news. Dante will be a free man. We just got a confession from Elyse's father." He stood up to shake my hand.

"What a great turn of events for our client. Elyse that

partnership is yours if you want it." I took a seat and steadied myself to tell Bill about my addiction.

"Bill, you might want to hold off on that partnership." He had a puzzled look on his face.

"What's the matter Savannah?"

"Bill, I will need a leave of absence. I need to handle a problem. I am a drug addict." The look on his face was one of disbelief.

"You are kidding me. No way; I would have known. Your work is impeccable. How could that be possible?" I wanted to crawl in a hole and disappear.

"I am a heroin addict and I have been for some time. I don't inject, I smoke it. Not that it makes a difference. I am finally going to seek out help and I need time to get myself together. I would understand if you want me to resign but for the first time in a long time, I have to take care of myself. I know you are disappointed and I am sorry."

"Savannah you are a top notch lawyer and I would not want to lose you. I am not disappointed; shocked, yes! What do you need from me? When you are ready, your job is still here waiting for you. You can also trust me to be discreet about this and I will keep this between you and I. Anything you need, please just ask." I did not expect Bill to be so understanding.

"I truly appreciate your understanding. I will update you along that way." He got up and came over and gave me a hug. We said our goodbyes and I left. My next stop was Rikers Island to give Dante the good news. As I drove out to Rikers I could not help but think, was I about to let a murder back out into the streets? I was hired to represent Dante in the murder of Elyse and I have to fulfill my obligation but does my obligation end there?

I was in the waiting room and I could hear the chains as Dante walked down the hall. When he got to the waiting room, he had a look of anticipation.

"Hi Ms. Taylor. I was hoping to see you before the trial started." I look at Dante and tried to read his face. All I could see was a defeated man. I could not see the face of a murderer.

"Dante, there will be no trial. You are free. Elyse's father confessed to murdering her." He had a look of disbelief on his face.

"Are you kidding me? Why would he do that to Elyse? Oh my God, this nightmare is over for me."

"Mr Daniels is not a well man, mentally. He was blaming Elyse for the death of his wife. I have submitted the paperwork signed by the Judge to have you processed out of here. Is there anyone that you want me to call?"

"You can call my brother. And tell him not to tell my parents because I want to surprise them." Even though I just gave him his freedom back there was sadness in his eyes.

"I understand how Mr. Daniels felt about losing his wife because I feel the same pain now with Elyse gone. But if we had a child, there is no way I could take my child's life. I understand that he has some mental issues but I just can't comprehend. Now that I am free, I feel like I am grieving all over again." I felt sorry for Dante even though I suspected him of being a serial killer.

"Will you get back to boxing now that this is over?"

"Yes, boxing will help keep my mind occupied. Thank you for all of your help."

"You are welcome Dante. Let me know the next time you are boxing and I might come and see you. Well I have to leave now, good luck." My gut instinct told me that our paths would cross again real soon.

When I got to my car, I called Jeffrey. His phone when straight to voicemail. I did not bother to leave a voicemail. I was already missing work. This was going to be a long journey. For Opioid addiction most facilities were in patient treatment. I decided to go to the Caron Treatment center. I was checking in tomorrow. Jeffrey agreed to go with me and I agreed to let him. I finally accepted that this was something I needed to do.

THE THREAT IS REAL

*D*elores was going to stay at the house to care for Nina while I was gone. I was scheduled to be gone for three months. I went in the room to say my goodbye to Nina.

"Hey sis, I am ready to leave. Delores has everything she needs. Call me whenever you need to and I will do the same." She reached for me and I went over and gave her a hug.

"You're going to get through this with flying colors. I will be fine so don't worry about me. I want you to focus on getting clean."

Jeffrey was out in his car waiting for me. I knew that three months was going to feel like a lifetime. When we got to the facility, there were a bunch of meetings and tours of the facility. When I finally got to my room, it was time to say goodbye to Jeffrey.

"Well I guess it is time to say goodbye. Jeffrey, thank you for everything you have done. I really like and appreciate the new Jeffrey. Please call me because I have a feeling I will be craving phone calls soon." He moved in closer to me.

"I will call you everyday until you tell me to stop. I know you will beat this and get back to being the best lawyer in New York city." I was already missing him. We hugged and kissed goodbye.

There I was all alone, just me and my addiction. My days were filled with medications, therapy and group therapy. I was not trying to socialize much but one lady latched on to me and I could not shake her. Her name was Kim and she was also addicted to heroin. She was nice but I really did not want to be bothered. I dealt with her because I did not want to hurt her feelings. After dinner was our reflection time. They encouraged us to journal. Instead of journaling, I used this time to do more research into the serial murders in Vegas. I was currently researching all of Dante's fights and their locations. I wanted to see if there were murders in other cities that he has fought in and if they are similar to the Vegas murders. He has fought in New York, New Jersey, California, Vegas and Florida. Now all I would need is for Jeffrey to check the police databases in each state to see if there were women murdered that had a cross carved into the shoulder.

My treatment was going well for the most part. I had a

couple rough nights but the meds they had me on helped take the edge off. I talked to Nina and Jeffrey almost every night. I called Derrick and he was more than happy to go to the library and get copies of the news articles about the murders. He sent me all the articles for all seven murders. We talk for almost an hour. Derrick was easy to talk to and I enjoyed his company. I did not tell him where I was and had no intentions. I was carefully reviewing each article and something caught my attention. The timeframe of one of the murders was around the same time that Dante would have been in the ring fighting. This did not make sense to me. Could the medical examiner have gotten the time of death wrong? I was not sure if this was just a minor oversight or should I be concerned. How could Dante murder this woman at the same time he was fighting?

Over the next week I was able to construct a timeline around the Vegas murders. One of the counselors was knocking on my door.

"Savannah, it Mrs. Nelson. I have a letter that came in the mail for you." I opened the door while wondering who would be sending me a letter.

"Hi Mrs. Nelson. Thank you." I took the letter and closed my door. I figured it had to be Jeffrey because who else, other than Nina and Bill, knew that I was here. I opened the letter and started reading it.

"*Savannah I have some important advice for you. Find a hobby and stay out of business that does not concern you. This a subtle warning and next time won't be so subtle. Sincerely, X marks the spot."*

What the hell? Who was this? Was this referring to the murders in Vegas? I grabbed my phone and immediately called Jeffrey.

"Hello."

"Hey Jeffrey. I just got this weird letter, I think it is a threat, but I am not sure." I read the letter to Jeffrey.

"Savannah, are you still snooping around those murders?" I did not want to lie to Jeffrey.

"Yes, but honestly not where anyone would know." He took a deep breath.

"Listen Savannah, this is serious and I need you to stop digging into this. I need you to promise because I don't want anything to happen to you. I will see what I can find out but you need to stay out of it." I had no intention of being scared off but I knew what I had to tell Jeffrey.

"I will back off." He wasn't buying it.

"Savannah, I am serious. Leave this alone."

"I hear you, besides what much can I do here in this place." Jeffrey knew me very well and he knew how stubborn I could be.

"I will see what I can find out and you concentrate on your recovery, understand."

"Understood. I will talk to you later." After talking with Jeffrey I was looking at the letter again. I was wondering if Dante sent this to me. There was no return address and nothing to link this to Dante. I wanted to call

Dante but I had no real reason to call him. I felt like my hands were tied being here in this facility. I was almost sure that Dante had to be behind this. The letter was typed so I could not compare handwriting. Along with my frustrations about this case I also was dealing with the urge to take a trip. This was turning out to be my roughest night here. What I did learn from my therapy was I used my addiction as a mechanism to escape my frustrations. My therapy sessions were teaching me how to deal with my frustrations. Unfortunately, tonight I wish I had some drugs other than what they were giving me. I needed the real deal. I could not sleep so I continued looking into other murders that coincided with Dante's boxing matches locations. Why was I so obsessed with this case? I could just walk away and no one would be wiser. But I constantly think about those innocent women who were murdered and someone has to be the voice for them. I finally was able to get a couple of hours sleep.

Thirty days into my treatment and I no longer craved heroin. I know the bigger test comes when I am no longer on any meds. Also when I throw in a stressful situation. Nina and Jeffrey called on a regular basis. Jeffrey did not mention the Vegas murders and neither did I. I saw in the news that Dante has a championship fight scheduled in 6 weeks. He was scheduled to fight in Vegas. I was curious to see if a murder would occur around that time. I wish I could prevent a murder from occurring but I really did not have any concrete evidence. Maybe if Dante thought I was into him, he would not commit a murder for fear of getting caught. That would be a dangerous game to play and Jeffrey would be really upset not to mention Nina too. I wish there was more I could do. I would be released from rehab 2 weeks before his fight. I took a shower and went to my therapy session. My therapist was a woman named Jessica Rollands. She was easy to talk to and I tried to really make the best of my sessions. I knocked on her office door.

"Come in Savannah and have a seat. How are things going today?"

This was her question everyday.

"Things are good." She opened up my file and smiled at me.

"I have some good news today. Starting tomorrow morning we will be taking you off all of your drugs. Your last month we will focus on coping mechanisms without the assistance of drugs. If it becomes difficult at any point we can always provide some medication as needed. The ultimate goal is for you to be completely drug free for a month before being released. Do you have any questions?" I was ready to do this.

"No I don't have any questions about what you just told me but I did want to run something by you. What if you suspected someone was doing something harmful to someone else but you did not have any proof. And then you thought they were about to harm someone else. What would you do?" She closed my file and removed her glasses.

"I would tell the authorities. If I am wrong it would be a little embarrassment but if I was right I could save someone from harm. Is there something you know that you want to talk about." I usually don't lie to Mrs. Rollands but I could not tell her what was going on.

"No, the question was for a friend. I told them the same thing." She gave me a knowing smile.

"Just remember I am here if you need to talk. I am proud of you; you have done a great job."

"Thank you Mrs. Rollands."

After therapy I went back to my room and I was checking my messages and there was a message from Derrick. I returned his call.

"Hello."

"Hey Derrick, I see you called. What's up?"

"I don't know if you heard but Dante has a fight coming up and I was wondering if you would like to come up for the weekend and check out his fight. We could go out to dinner and celebrate. What do you say?" This was a perfect excuse to be near Dante.

"I would love to come to Vegas for the fight." He hesitated because I don't think he expected me to say yes.

"Wonderful and I will pay for your flight and hotel."

"That is not necessary." I did not want him to think I owed him anything.

"No strings attached and I will not take no for an answer." He was not going to get an argument from me.

"No argument here." I was glad I would be seeing him again.

"Looking forward to seeing you again. I remember what you told me and I am not putting any pressure on you but I do enjoy your company. I will email you the plane and hotel information once I book them. Are you going to stay Friday to Monday?"

"That will be fine. I will talk with you soon."

We hung up and then I realize that Jeffrey might not be too keen on the idea of me spending the weekend in Vegas with another man. Even though I would not be staying with him, in Jeffrey's eyes I was spending the weekend with this man. Jeffrey and I were not officially dating but I knew how he felt about me and by no means did I want to lead him on. I was developing feelings for him but I was not sure if I was ready for a commitment. I also enjoy talking with Derrick and if I was honest with myself, I believe I was developing feelings for him also. I am sitting here in rehab trying to get my life together while complicating it more. I thought about being totally drug free tomorrow. It was slightly scary but I was confident that I would be fine. I have to admit, even though I enjoyed getting high, the thought of being clean was exhilarating. For the first time I pulled out my journal and started writing. I wrote about my fears:

All too often people look at successful people and think to themselves that life is grand for them. They do not realize that we hurt, bleed and suffer pain the same as anyone else. The only difference is we become experts at hiding these things. When our lives are lonely and empty, we fill it with non-stop work. When we are hurting, instead of seeking out someone to talk to, we put on the appearance of strength. And like so many I turned to artificial comfort. An escape from reality to a place of no fears or worries. We don't want to see the real damage we are doing ourselves. Just looking for instant gratification and nothing more. I am now ready to deal with the difficult days of life. I know everyday can't be a bed of roses. I also realize that I am stronger than I give myself credit for. I can start living for the first time in my life.

It felt so good to write and it felt therapeutic. I decided for the next month, I would write a little bit each night. Just as I was closing my journal, my phone rang.

"Hello?"

"So you did not get my letter or are you just ignoring my warning?" I did not recognize the voice because it sounded like it was being disguised.

"Who is this?"

"Don't worry about that. You need to back off or suffer the consequences. I promise that you don't know the meaning of suffering. Back off!!" The phone line went dead.

So this person has decided to step up their threats. But

who knew that I was looking into these murders. The only ones that knew were Nina, Jeffrey and I did mention it to Derrick. Could Derrick have mentioned it to Dante? I picked up my phone to call Derrick. He answered on the first ring.

"Hello."

"Derrick, this is Savannah. I need to know if you mentioned my theory about the Vegas murders to Dante?" He did not hesitate in answering my question.

"Of course not; I would have never mentioned that to Dante. Like I told you, we are not bosom buddies. Is something wrong?" I did not want to tell him about the note or phone call.

"No, I just wanted to make sure."

"Do you still think he is involved?" I need to steer this conversation in a different direction.

"Actually I don't think he is involved. They have another lead in the case. So I am moving on to a new case."

"Well looking forward to seeing you soon." We said our goodbyes. I believed Derrick and I don't think he mentioned anything to Dante. I was left wondering who called me. I was not going to let this person intimidate me.

Today was my drug free day. I was surprisingly nervous about being drug free. My phone rang and I already knew it was either Nina or Jeffrey.

"Hello."

"Hey Savanna, I just wanted to check on you before I went to work. You got this and if you need to talk for any reason, please call me." Jeffrey was so sweet and thoughtful.

"Thank you Jeffrey. I will admit, I am feeling a little nervous. But I got this and I am ready to take my life back."

"I am confident that you will be fine". I decided to tell him about my phone call.

"I got another threat but this time it was a phone call."

"Savanna you promised that you would leave the investigation to me." That was hard for me to do but I would never let him know that.

"I have not been investigating anymore. Plus who would know that I was checking into those murders? I am not letting anyone intimidate me."

"Listen Savanna, this is serious. I need you to call me immediately if you get another call or letter, understand?"

"I will call you right away. Can you stop by my house to see how Nina is doing? I know she is in good hands with Delores but just want her to see a different face."

"No problem; I will stop by during my lunch break. Listen I have to go; I will call you later."

"Ok. Talk to you later." I forgot to ask Jeffrey if there were any similar murders in other cities. I decided to wait until he called me later.

HARD TO SAY GOODBYE

*J*ust as I was settling in to start journaling, my phone rang.

"Hello." All I could hear was sobbing.

"Nina, is that you? Are you alright?" She was pulling herself together.

"Savannah, it's mom and dad." What was going on? I was scared to ask.

"What about mom and dad?" She choked back tears.

"They are dead. Killed in a car accident." I felt like I could not breathe. I could not believe what I was hearing.

"Savannah, there is more. The brake line on their car was cut. It is being ruled a murder." At this point Nina lost it. I had no consoling words because I was numb all over.

"Nina, I am leaving and will be home soon." I hung up

and fell to the floor. I curled up into a ball and cried so hard my chest was hurting.

I finally sat up on the floor beside my bed. Nina said murder and it dawned on me that this was my fault. This must have something to do with the murders in Vegas. I will make sure Dante pays for this and all of those other murders. I started packing my bags when there was a knock at my door. I opened the door and it was Mrs Rollands and Jeffrey.

"Savannah, I assume you heard the news." I guess she made that assumption because I was packing my bags.

"Savannah, I am so sorry about your parents. I just want you to know that we are here for you." I knew what her concern was.

"Don't worry Mrs Rollands I am not running off and getting high." Jeffery came over to hug me but I pushed him away. Mrs Rollands left us alone.

"You know this is my fault." I could not stop the tears from rolling and this time I did not push him away. He held me as I released all the hurt and anger.

"Listen, we will catch who did this. I am going to take you home. I will help you and Nina make all the arrangements. I know this is going to be hard but I promise I will be by your side."

Over the next couple of days I did not remember much; it was all a blur. We have a lot of family come into town and I felt like a Zombie moving around. Jeffrey was right there every step of the way. He did not pressure me to talk about my feelings, but he was just close enough to let me know he was there to listen if needed. It was the night before the funeral and Nina and I finally got a moment alone.

"How are you holding up Nina?" She smiles and reaches for my hand and holds it for a moment.

"This was not our fault. You investigating a murder case was something mom and dad would have encouraged you to do. They always taught us if you saw something wrong have the courage to make it right. When we lose a loved one I think it is natural to want to blame yourself. Fault only lies at the feet of the criminal responsible for this. We will get through this together and we will let the cops find the person responsible." I still felt guilty regardless of what Nina said.

"I keep thinking to myself that I may have defended our parents' murderer." I want to see Dante and look him in his eyes and see if he would flinch. Would I be able to see his guilt? And if it wasn't Dante, then who could it be."

"Savannah the truth is, we don't know if it is Dante and as a lawyer you know that you are innocent until proven guilty. We have to focus on laying mom and dad to rest tomorrow and sewing our lives back together. The person responsible will pay."

"Nina, I am going to Vegas next month to see Derrick." I waited for a response.

"But what about Jeffrey?"

"I am not going for social reasons. Dante has a fight

schedule and Derrick invited me to attend." Nina had a look of caution on her face.

"Be careful because you may be playing with fire. I wish I could go with you. I just want you to be careful because if Dante is onto you, there is no telling what he will do. Does Jeffrey know about this trip?"

"No he does not. I am trying to figure out a way to tell him. I know he is going to hit the ceiling but I don't want to keep secrets from him. The other problem is I actually enjoy being with Derrick and I feel guilty because I know Jeffrey is looking for more from our relationship." I was hoping that Nina had the secret answer.

"Savannah, if you have any intention of taking your relationship with Jeffrey any further, then you need to commit to that and not flirt with any other men that might evoke feelings. Derrick wants more than a friendship from you and he is going to try everything in his power to sway you. Be careful because you could get hurt along with hurting Jeffrey." I knew that everything she was telling me was true.

"You are right and I need to sit down and have a heart to heart conversation with Jeffrey." I sat on the edge of Nina's bed and gave her a big hug. I called Jeffrey and told him that we needed to talk after the funeral.

The funeral was hard but our parents were beautiful. It was so hard looking at them lying in those coffins. I was waiting to wake up from this nightmare. The church was packed, standing room only. So many people had nothing but wonderful things to say about our parents. Jeffrey was right there; my rock and my support. After everyone left, it was just Nina, Jeffrey and I. The house was so quiet and lonely.

"Jeffrey, can we go in my room to talk?" He got up and followed me into my room. He sat on the edge of my bed and I stood.

"What's up Savannah? Is something wrong?" I took a deep breath and sat next to him on the bed.

"No but I have not been totally honest with you and I don't want to keep things from you. I have not stopped looking into the murders in Vegas." He interrupted me;

"I know you haven't. Plus I did have some more news for you. I looked into the other places that Dante fought and there were no cold cases and no murders that fit the MO of the Vegas murders. So it looks like the murders were confined to Vegas." That was not what I wanted to hear.

"Well there is more; I also went on a dinner date with Derrick while in Vegas. I let him know that I was not looking for a relationship. He also called me a couple of days ago to invite me to Vegas for the weekend. He got tickets to Dante's upcoming fight. I am sure you know my motive behind accepting the invite." He looked disappointed.

"No I don't. What was your motive?"

"I wanted to get closer to Dante to see if I could

uncover something." He had a slight look of doubt on his face.

"Are you sure that was all? I have to be honest with you Savannah; I have taken steps to change my life around first and foremost for myself, but also for you. I never stopped loving you and I know my past behavior gives you every reason to not trust me but I am working hard to prove myself to you. I know you are free to see whomever you wish but I just want a chance." When I thought about it, I never stopped loving Jeffrey, I just hated what he became when he drank.

"Listen, I have enjoyed the new you and looking forward to seeing where this takes us." He had a look of discovery on his face.

"I have an idea; cancel your weekend with Derrick. I have plenty of vacation time. I will book a trip and get tickets to the fight. You can go with me and I can keep my eyes on you to make sure you stay out of trouble. I will book two rooms." At that very moment I realized that I wanted a future with Jeffrey.

"You only have to book one room." We both smiled and he leaned in for a kiss.

After Jeffrey left, I called Derrick.

"Hello."

"Hi Derrick, this is Savannah." I hated making this call.

"What's up pretty lady? Guess where I am?" Ok, I suppose I would play his guessing game.

"Where are you?" He sounded like a little kid at Christmas time.

"I am in New York. I have been here for a week on business. I was going to surprise you but you beat me to the punch." He was not making this easy.

"I am so sorry but I will need to cancel. I want to be totally honest with you. I am coming to Vegas that weekend but my ex-boyfriend and I have decided to work on our relationship. I am so sorry." There was a brief uncomfortable silence.

"I thought you did not want to get into a relationship with anyone."

I was about to answer and the phone line went dead. Did he just hang up on me? Wow, I was not expecting that type of reaction. I could not believe he just hung up without saying anything else. I knocked on Nina's door.

"Are you sleeping?"

"No, come in." She was reading a book and it looks like she had been crying.

"Are you ok sis?"

"I just was thinking about mom and dad. It just got so overwhelming, but I am ok now. What did you want?" I really felt bad bothering her at this moment.

"Don't worry, come sit down and talk to me." I sat on the edge of her bed.

"I had that heart to heart with Jeffrey and it went well. I told him everything and I am going with him to the fight in Vegas. So I decided to call Derrick and be honest with him. Well I explained about cancelling and working on my relationship with my ex-boyfriend. He just hung up on me without another word."

"What? Wow, I think he was falling hard for you. Watch out because he might start stalking you." We looked at each other and burst out laughing. We needed the laughter right at that moment.

"Savannah, I believe Derrick was really into you and he was hurt."

"I know but I just did not figure him as the type that would react that way. I thought he would appreciate me being honest with him." We spent the night talking and reminiscing about mom and dad.

I did not return to the rehab center. I was in control and I had a support partner if I had the urge. I called my counselor daily and I went to an outpatient support group. I did not go back to work right away. Jeffrey was by my side every step of the way and he never pressured me for nothing more than I was willing to give. Nina and I helped each other as we grieved our parents. It was Saturday and Jeffrey was in the kitchen making dinner. Jeffrey loved to cook and I love the fact that he loved to cook. I was sitting at the kitchen table watching him as he cooked.

"Jeffrey, has there been any progress into my parents murder?" Jeffrey was not directly involved with the investigation but his buddies keep him up to date with the case.

"Nothing new; there were no fingerprints and no one saw anyone by their car."

"Jeffrey, do you think this has anything to do with the threat I got from Dante?" He came over and sat down next to me.

"Listen sweetheart, we don't know or have proof that Dante is the one that threatened. I am not sure this is related to the threats but to be honest, it is possible." He saw the look on my face.

"Savannah, do not blame yourself. You can't do that to yourself." That was easier said than done. If I didn't snoop around into those Vegas murders, my mom and dad might still be alive.

"I can't help it but I will try not to let it consume me." I grabbed him by the hand and pulled him in for a kiss. He leaned back and looked me in my eyes. "I love you Savannah and I want to spend the rest of my life with you" He reaches in his pocket and pulls out a little black velvet box. I could not believe that he was about to propose to me. I did not see this coming and I was filled with anxiety as he got down on one knee.

"Savannah Taylor, would you do me the honor of being my wife?" I was speechless for a few moments. Finally, I found the words;

"Yes I will marry you Jeffrey." We embraced and kissed. There was so much passion and fire in that kiss. I don't think I ever truly stopped loving Jeffrey, I just hated who he was when he drank.

"Nina, I have something to show you and tell you!" I yelled from the kitchen.

"Just get in here and let me see the ring!"

"You told her already?" He laughed,

"Who do you think helped me pick the ring?" I then stopped for a moment as I thought about my parents. It did not feel right to be so happy at this moment. Jeffrey knew what I was feeling.

"Savannah, your parents would want you to be happy." Despite all that has happened, I was very happy. I was headed to show Nina my ring when my phone rang.

"Hello." There was a slight pause and heavy breathing.

"I am so sorry to hear about your parents." The person on the other end sounded like their voice was muffled or like they were trying to disguise their voice.

"Who is this?"

"You do know that this is all on you. You are the reason they are gone!" I dropped the phone and Jeffrey came running out of the kitchen.

"What's the matter?" I could not talk, I just fell into his arms and began crying. He just held me until I pulled myself together. We went into Nina's room because she was calling out to see what was wrong. I sat on the edge of her bed.

"Savannah, what is wrong?"

"It was him again. He was saying it was my fault that

our parents are dead." Jeffrey kneeled down in front of me.

"I am going to put a tail on Dante. Unfortunately, I don't have enough to bring him in and I don't want to spook him. As for you, my future wife, I will be keeping a very close eye on you. And remember you are not responsible for your parents death."

"Hey guys, I have a surprise, that might brighten things up around here. Delores, you can bring it in now." Delores entered the room pushing a wheelchair. Nina grabbed her right leg and swung over to the side of the bed and she did the same with her left leg. I watched as she maneuvered herself into the wheelchair with the big smile on her face. This was the best news of the day. I was so proud of Nina and how determined she was about not giving up.

VEGAS

It was time for our trip to Vegas. I had not gotten any more calls. I was packing my bags and looking forward to spending time with Jeffrey. Jeffrey had a guy following Dante but he had nothing out of the ordinary to report. My phone rang and I did not recognize the phone number. I started not to answer the call but I gave into my need to know.

"Hello."

"So are you packed and ready to go?" This was not Jeffrey.

"Why are you calling me?"

"Just wanted you to know how excited I am that we will be in Vegas at the same time. I will be busy, killing and branding a few women. But here is something for you to think long and hard about. Get into my business and your boyfriend will be a thing of your past. I will take everything that you love slowly and painfully. Stay out of my business. You know what I am capable of and you have suffered enough hurt and pain of the last couple of months. Let your parents be the last tragedy in your life."

This time he hung up before I could. I was shaken but not deterred. I definitely was not going to tell Jeffrey about this call because he would be cancelling our trip without a doubt. I was not going to miss a chance at seeing this monster sent to death row. Then I thought, if it is not Dante, then who could it be and what was I getting myself into. I could not let this go because of my parents. My phone rang again and this time I recognized the number.

"Hey Jeffrey."

"Hey Savannah, just checking to see if you are all packed and ready. I will pick you up in the morning around 6 am." Hearing his voice was comforting.

"I will be ready." I could not imagine something happening to Jeffrey. I was sure of one thing; I love Jeffrey.

"Love you pretty lady and see you in the morning."

"Love you too." I hung up and for the first time since I got home from rehab, I thought of taking a trip. Instead, I took a long hot shower and went to bed. I did not sleep well because I really wanted to get high. I had not felt this way in awhile and for the first time I understood what it meant to be a drug addict. I thought about calling Devon but I refused to give in to the demon. Instead I called Mrs. Rollands and we talked for more than an hour. I felt much better after talking to her.

"Thank you Mrs. Rollands for taking my call so late at night but I just needed someone to talk to and I did not want to give in to my desire."

"Savannah, call me anytime you need to talk. That is what I am here for and I am so proud of your progress. Get some rest and have a safe trip to Vegas."

Jeffrey arrived promptly and we headed to the airport.

"You seem to be distant this morning. Are you ok?" I could not stop thinking about that last call that I got.

"I am fine, just a little tired because I did not sleep well last night." We were at the airport park garage.

"Are you feeling ok?" I was not in a sharing mood at the moment.

"I am just fine. Looking forward to Vegas."

We parked the car and got the shuttle to our terminal. We had thirty minutes before we boarded our plane. While waiting for the plane to board, I checked my email. There was an email with the subject line, "stay out of my business." I immediately clicked on the email to see what the message was and the same text that was in the subject line was also in the body of the email and that was all. I didn't want anything to happen to Jeffrey or anybody else that I loved, but there was this need to know. I keep thinking about all of those women that were murdered and I felt it was my responsibility to bring this murderer to justice.

Our flight was uneventful and we arrived in Vegas around 12:30 pm. The fight was going to be at the MGM Grand so that's where we booked our room. We were in the West Wing King suite in the west tower.

"Wow Jeffrey, this is a beautiful room." He walked up behind me and put his arms around my waist.

"You deserve nothing but the best. I am going to spoil you." I turned around to face him.

"I notice there is only one bed." He gently took my hand and led me to the bed. We both sat down.

"Savannah, I love you and I am so sorry for how I treated you in the past. I wish I could erase the past. I have taken time to understand Jeffrey and work on me. This was so important because I want to give you the best of me. No I would be lying if I said, I didn't want to make love to you every night that we are here. But the truth is I don't want to start out that way. I want to get to know you before becoming intimate. I am ok with spending the next couple of nights just holding you. I want to listen to and feel your heartbeat. And when we do make love, it will be an experience beyond measure." This was the man that I was sure I wanted to marry.

"Jeffrey, let's get married here in Vegas!" He had a look of total disbelief on his face.

"Are you sure about that?"

"I am as sure as I will ever be. The fight is Saturday

night, so let's get married on Sunday." I could see the excitement building in Jeffrey.

"What about Nina? Do you think she would be upset that she was not part of our wedding?" I had not thought about Nina, but he had a valid concern.

"I will call her and tell her what our plans are and feel her out. If she is upset we will wait. Does that work for you?" He leaned over and gently kissed me.

"I am here to stay so now or later, I am good with it." I picked up my phone.

"I am going to call her now." Her phone rang three times before she picked up.

"Hey Nina, are you ok?" She sounded like she was asleep.

"I was just taking a nap. How are you guys doing and how is Vegas?"

"We are great and I wanted to ask you something. If I eloped would you be upset with me?" Nina started laughing.

"No but when you get home we would have to plan a formal wedding. So a Vegas wedding?" I looked at Jeffrey and gave him the thumbs up.

"Nina, I am so happy and I want to marry Jeffrey now. We could definitely plan a big spectacular wedding when I get home. Are you sure you are not upset?"

"Girl please, I am so happy for you and him. See if you can have the ceremony videotaped. What day will it happen?"

"It will be Sunday, but I will call you and give you all the details. Right now, I am going to the mall to see if I can find a dress." I was so glad that Nina was happy for me.

"I will talk to you later and Nina, thank you and love you."

"Love you too!"

"So we are going to the mall?" I looked at Jeffrey like he was crazy.

"We? No not we, but me. You can't be with me while I get my dress. That is bad luck!" He chuckled and drew me in for a long kiss.

"That's why I love you so much. Well, while you are gone, I am going to take a shower and when you get back, we can go to dinner."

"That's a plan and I won't take too long. I am taking an Uber over to Meadows Mall." As I was walking to the elevator, I almost bumped into someone. When I looked up, it was Dante.

"Hey Ms. Taylor, what are you doing in Vegas?" This was awkward but I thought quickly.

"I'm here to see you." He had a puzzled look on his face.

"To see you fight." He started smiling.

"Wow, this is great. I am glad you came. Are you alone?"

"No, I came with my fiance." He looked sincerely glad to see me.

"I owe you so much for what you did for me."

"You don't owe me anything. I was just doing my job."
He had a sudden look like a light bulb just went on.

 "I would love for you and your fiance to be my guest
at ringside." I did not feel like I was having a conversation
with a murderer but I felt sure that Dante was a killer.

"That is very generous of you and I will take you up on
your offer. My fiance would love ringside seats."

"That is great and I will leave the tickets for you at the
front desk."

 "Thank you Dante and good luck tomorrow night."

"Thank you Ms Taylor." As I was walking away I
turned around.

"Dante, please call me Savannah." He smiled and went
his way. I was so caught up in Jeffrey that I almost forgot
why I had really come to Vegas. I was not expecting to run
into Dante but for some reason I felt like he could not be a
murderer. But I had to remember that some of the more
infamous murderers were experts in deceiving people.

When I got to the mall, my first stop was Lord and
Taylor. Within ten minutes I found the perfect dress. It
was cream colored and very elegant. I would worry about
a wedding gown when we had our ceremony back home
with family and friends. I got back from the mall around 3
o'clock and headed to our room. The closer I got to the
room the more I had an eerie feeling like something was
wrong. I quickened my pace and when I got to the room

the door was open. That wasn't like Jeffrey to leave the door. I rushed into the room.

"Jeffrey are you here?" I looked in the bathroom and there was no sign of Jeffrey. I took a deep breath. Maybe he went down to the casino. But why would he leave the door open. There was a note taped on the television. I ran over and grabbed the note.

"I told you to stay out of my business. Game on and no police or else Jeffrey will need to be fitted for a coffin."

I sunk down to the floor and all I could do was cry. This was all my fault and now Jeffrey was in danger. I did not know what to do. I took a deep breath and tried to gather my composure. I decided I was going to confront Dante. I needed to make him understand that he needed to stop what he was doing. Sounded simple enough but I knew that was not the case. I needed to figure out a way to find out his room number. Then I remember that Dante was leaving me tickets at the front desk. I grabbed my purse and went down to the front desk. I was waiting in line and guess who walked through the lobby. I ran over to Dante;

"Hey Dante, can we talk in private for a moment." He was with his entourage.

"Sure, is something wrong?"

"Can we go to your room?" He dismissed his entourage and we went up to his room. He was staying in an Executive suite. His room was twice the size of our room.

"Ms Taylor, what's up?" I was not sure how to approach him so I decided to be straight forward.

"Dante I know about the girls and I know you have Jeffrey. I don't want you to harm him and I promise I will walk away and never say a word. Please let Jeffrey go." He was looking at me as if I was a crazy woman.

"Ms. Taylor, what the hell are you talking about? Do you need me to call someone?" He looked like he didn't understand what I was talking about.

"I know all about the murders. There is no need to pretend you don't know what I am talking about. I know about your calling card. You carved an X on all of you victims."   Dante went to pick up his phone and I ran over and knocked it out of his hand.

"I need to get you some help Ms Taylor!" I looked Dante in the eyes and I realized that he really did not know what I was talking about.

"Can I sit down and explain everything to you?" I explain everything to Dante from the very beginning. I was desperate and I just needed to trust someone.

"Ms Taylor."

"Please call me Savannah."

"Savannah, I understand why you thought that I was a murderer but you need to go to the police."

"I can't because that would jeopardize Jeffrey's life. I

need to figure out who this is and what they want." Dante sat down next to me.

"Listen I will help in any way that I can but I can't do anything until after my fight tomorrow night. I have to get focused on my fight."

I couldn't expect him to risk his fight for me. I felt lost and alone at this moment. All I could think about right now was getting high. I was glad I was in Vegas because I did not know where to cop drugs. If I was home I am not sure how strong I could be.

"Listen I have a friend here that might be able to help. I think you met him. His name is Derrick. Didn't you speak with him." Didn't want to hear that name.

"I don't think Derrick would be willing to help me."

"Savannah, Derrick is cool and I am sure he would help." I guess I should let Dante know about Derrick and I.

"I went on a date with Derrick. I was really into him but I had unfinished business with my ex. I tried to explain but he hung up on me. So I doubt he would be willing to help." He chuckled.

"Under the circumstances I believe he would put his feelings aside to help. Let me talk to him and see what he says. He knows Vegas better than you or I so he might be a good resource. Go back to your room and I will contact you shortly."

"But what do I do in the meantime?"

"Just go back to your room and hopefully this person will contact you. I will reach out to Derrick right away. As hard as it is, please try to stay calm. We need to find out what he wants. I will help you but you need to stay calm. I will call you after I talk to Derrick." I left and went back to my room. I did not know what to do. I felt so helpless.

13

CLARITY

I checked my phone and there was a message from Nina's doctor. I wonder what he wanted? I dialed the phone number that he left on the message. Just as I realized the time difference, Dr. Lawrence answered with a groggy voice. "Dr Lawrence, this is Savannah Taylor and I apologize for calling so late. I am in Vegas and I did not think about the time difference." "Please no apology needed. It is really not that late, I just was catching a quick nap. I guess you are returning my call. I just wanted to know if you or Nina would be picking up her medication or did you want me to have it dropped off to your house?"

"If you could drop it at the house, that would be great. Thank you and have a good evening."

I hung up and suddenly something he said caught my attention, He said did I or Nina want to pick up her medication. That was odd because how did he expect Nina to get to his office when she was wheelchair bound. I suppose he really wasn't thinking clearly, especially since I woke him from his sleep. I will call Nina tomorrow and check on her. In the meantime, all I could think about was Jeffrey. Was he hurt or was he still alive? This was all my fault. If I had left this alone and let the police investigate the murders then Jeffrey would be ok. What made me think that I could solve this case. I was ready to accuse the wrong man of murder. I was so sure that it was Dante. Now I had no idea who was behind the murders and kidnapping of Jeffrey. My phone was ringing.

"Hello, who is this?"

"Hey Savannah, this is Dante. Derrick has agreed to help. He will be over in 30 mins so meet me in my room. Have you heard anything yet?"

"Nothing and that is making me nervous. Are you sure that we can trust Derrick? He was pretty upset with me."

"This is a serious matter and Derrick is not that petty. See you in 30 minutes."

The 30 minutes were the longest of my life. Just as I was about to leave my room, my phone rang. My heartbeat sped up and my hand started shaking as I picked up the phone.

"Hello." The voice on the other end was very muffled but I could understand it.

"Be at 924 North 4th street in 2 hours. No police or

your boyfriend is dead." I wanted to keep him talking to see if I could learn something about him.

"How do I know that he is still alive? And what do you want from me?" There was a long pause.

"Two hours and don't be late." He hung up the phone. I rushed out of my room and headed to Dante's room. I knocked on Dante's room door. He opened the door and gestured for me to come into his room. There was Derrick sitting on the couch. This was an awkward moment but I needed his help.

"Hey Derrick, thanks for your help. I know things.." He quickly interrupted me.

"No need to go on. Have you heard anything yet?"

"I got a phone call just before I came here. All he said was, "be at 924 North 4th street in 2 hours. No police or your boyfriend is dead." Derek was sitting down, so I walked over to the couch and sat down also.

"I know that area of town. It is called the cultural corridor. Not a very safe part of town. I can go with you. I would not want you going to that side of town by your-self." Dante interrupted.

"Listen guys, I have a press conference I need to get to so I am going to leave. You are in good hands with Derrick. Be very careful."

We all got up to leave. When we got to the lobby Dante went a different direction for his press conference. I felt slightly awkward with Derrick but he seemed to not be holding any grudges.

"Hey Savannah, have you eaten today?" I did not realize it but I had not eaten since breakfast.

"I have not eaten since breakfast. Too nervous to think about eating."

"Well we have over an hour and half before we have to go to that address, so let go and get something to eat."

"I am not sure I can eat right now." He grabbed me gently by the arm.

"I insist because you have to take care of yourself and I am sure your boyfriend would agree with me. We don't have to go to a sit down restaurant, we can just go through a drive thru just to get something in your stomach." He was right because I was very hungry. We stopped at Wendy's and the drive thru line was very long.

"Listen, I will go inside. What do you want?" I did not want to get a lot because I know my nerves would not allow me to eat all my food.

"Just get me a Dave's single with cheese and a medium strawberry lemonade." I thought for a second how lucky I was to have Derrick helping me.

He was gone for about 10 minutes. He got back with the food and I woofed down that burger. I was hungrier than I realized. I was halfway through my strawberry lemonade when all of a sudden I started getting dizzy and I felt like I was going to pass out.

"Derrick, I feel strange. What's happening to me?" Last thing I remembered was Derrick smiling at me.

When I woke up my head was hurting. I was sitting on

the floor in an empty room. I went to move and that is when I noticed I was chained at the ankle and the chain was attached to a radiator. Last thing I could remember was eating at Wendy's with Derrick. I was definitely confused. I yelled out.

"Help me!! Is there anyone here? Hello!!!" The door to the room slowly opened and Derrick walked through.

"Derrick what is going on?" He smiled and sat down in a chair that was facing me.

"When my partner gets here you will start to see things more clearly. You see life is about paying your dues. And it is time you pay your bill. First let's talk about the murders; you see you did a good job at solving those murders. Any good detective would follow the same leads and you would land at Dante's front door." He looked like he was enjoying every moment of this and I was not quite sure what this was.

"Derrick, do you know something about those murders?" He sat back in his chair and smiled.

"Dante does not have the balls to murder anyone but I made sure all the evidence pointed to him."

"You are the murder? Why would you kill those innocent women?" He sat up in his chair, seemingly a little agitated.

"Unfortunately, they were just casualties of war. You see Dante took something very special from me and I could never forgive him for that. Elyse meant the world to me and he took her from me. Do you know how hard it was for me to pretend to be friends with him? At first I thought about just killing him but then that would be too quick and I wanted him to suffer. I wanted to take something from him. Freedom is a prized possession and what better revenge than taking his freedom away. It took many years to plan this out but then Elyse's father loses his mind and kills Elyse. I have something for daddy dearest soon but I must take care of Dante, your boyfriend and you first." This was madness and I needed to find a way to get out of this mess.

"Where is Jeffrey?"

"He is in the other room. He is a little drugged up but he is fine for now. He put up a good fight but I won in the end. You know when I met you, I actually thought about walking away from all of this because I thought you were different but I was so wrong. You had no problem leading me on and dropping me so quick when the next man came along."

"Derrick, I didn't mean to lead you on and I am sorry if I hurt you." He laughed and got up in my face.

"It is too late for sorry. I see why your sister resents you."

"You don't know anything about my sister or our relationship." He smiled and I heard the front door open. A few moments later she walked through the door and I felt lightheaded as if I was going to faint. She walked without the assistance of a wheelchair.

"Nina, what is going on?" I was in a state of shock.

She smiled at me but it was not a loving smile; it was a devious and sinister smile.

"I know you have so many questions and they will be answered in due time. You see sister dear, for the first time, I have the upper hand. I have lived in your shadow for too many years. Yes, it was a miraculous recovery. Walking and keeping it from you was easy because as always, you are so consumed with yourself." I could not believe what I was hearing and seeing.

"But I took you in and I cared for you. I have done nothing but try to love you. How could you deceive me like this?" Nina was void of any compassion or love.

"I hate you Savannah and I have hated you all my life. I was so sick of our parents always comparing me to you. I am my own person, and they failed to realize that." It suddenly dawned on me; Nina was responsible for our parents' death.

"Oh my God, you killed our parents! You are sick!"

"No I did not kill our parents, I killed your parents." Nina was delusional and hell bent on destroying me and anyone attached to me.

"So now you are going to kill me and Jeffrey?" She smiled and walked closer.

"Yes, I am going to make sure Jeffrey goes first and you will watch as life leaves his body. I want you to suffer." I was so defeated at this moment. I did not care what happened to me. I was so sorry that Jeffrey was dragged into this.

"Nina, Jeffrey has nothing to do with this, so please spare his life." She laughed and pulled over a chair and sat right in front of me.

"Oh you are so wrong. He has a piece of your heart and that makes him part of this. Now get comfy because you will not know when death will visit. I am going to give you a little time to think things over and I am going to have Derrick bring in your lover boy." Derrick left the room and about 5 minutes later he returned with Jeffrey. Jeffrey's left eye was swollen and his lip was swollen and bloody. It was apparent that Derrick worked him over real good. I never felt so helpless while tears streamed down my face. Jeffrey's arms were tied behind his back and Derrick put a chain on his ankle and chained him to a pole on the opposite side of the room. Derrick and Nina left the room.

"Jeffrey are you ok?"

"Savannah I am ok. A little beat up but I am ok. Did they hurt you?"

"No, at least not physically. I honestly believed that Nina and I had made a connection. She seemed so sincere. I am so sorry Jeffrey." Jeffrey smiled at me.

"Savannah do not be hard on yourself. You did the best you could do and you are not responsible for your sister. We have to focus on trying to get out of here. I have a pocket knife in my back pocket. I was waiting for an opportunity to try and get at it and now is the time. I am not sure how long we have but that is our best shot at this time."

"But you are forgetting that your feet are chained and Derrick has the key." Jeffrey did not let that detail stop him from trying. He was working non-stop at getting the knife and cutting the ropes that were around his hands. After 20 minutes Jeffrey's hands were free.

"What now Jeffrey?" He was thinking.

"When they return I will act like my hands are still tied until I find the opportunity to get the drop on them. Savannah I did not wait this long to ask for your hand in marriage and then lose you. We are going to have the big wedding and I am going to spend the rest of my life making you happy. How are you doing over there?"

"You will never believe this but I am hungry." We both burst out laughing. How were we able to laugh? At this time all we had was each other. For the next hour we just talk about our past, present and our future. We heard footsteps and Derrick walk through the door. ""How are the love birds doing?" I did not see Nina.

"Where is Nina?" He was standing by Jeffrey and I wanted to keep him engaged in conversation so Jeffrey could make his move.

"Don't worry your sister will be joining us soon. She would not miss the ending to this story for nothing in the world." I needed to buy Jeffrey more time by keeping Derrick distracted.

"Derrick I am hungry. Even men on death row get a final meal. You think I could get something to eat?" Just as Derrick was about to move in my direction, Jeffrey made his move. He wrestled Derrick to the ground and a struggle ensued. They struggled for about 3 to 4 minutes until Jeffrey was able to get Derrick in a head lock and within seconds he snapped his neck. He quickly got the keys from Derrick's pocket and removed the chains from both our legs. He helped me up and just as we were about to make our escape, all I heard was a gunshot. I watched as Jeffrey dropped to the floor. Nina shot Jeffrey and something came over me. I lunged at Nina and we both went down on the floor and fought for the gun. We struggled for about 2 minutes until I heard another gunshot. I was not sure if it was Nina or me that took the bullet. Then Nina slumped over and fell into my arms. She looked up at me with a smile on her face.

"You always win in the end. I will no longer walk in your shadow." She closed her eyes. I quickly got up and rushed to Jeffrey.

"Jeffrey are you ok?" He smiled at me with reassurance. "I took the bullet in my shoulder. I will be ok." I leaned in and gave him a passionate kiss.

"Jeffrey, I love you. Nina is gone. I don't think I ever truly knew my sister. I do hope she is at peace finally."

Derrick and I were busy planning our wedding. I was trying to adjust to life without my parents and my sister. I had a small private funeral for Nina and Jeffrey helped me with everything. It has been 7 months and things were starting to feel normal again. I started back to work and after a month Bill made me partner. My current case was a state senator that was accused of murdering his wife. It felt good to be working again. Jeffrey and I were living together.

"Hey beautiful since we both have the day off, and you know that doesn't happen often, what do you want to do?" I was making breakfast and watching CNN news.

"I don't know so why don't you surprise me."

"Well I am going to take a quick shower before breakfast." When Jeffrey left the room I turned up the television to hear the news. There was a reporter talking;

"There have been 3 murders over the last six months in the Vegas area. All 3 victims were women. They were strangled and an X was carved in their shoulders. Serial killer strikes again in Vegas!"

ABOUT THE AUTHOR

Shannon Spruill was born and raised in Brooklyn, New York, but now resides in Buffalo, NY. She is a wife to Deacon Esau Spruill, Jr. and mother to three sons.

Shannon graduated Suma Cum Laude from Bryant and Stratton College with a bachelor's degree in Business Administration and a master's degree in Computer Information Systems from Boston University. She is currently working on her doctoral degree in Biblical Studies. She is an Account Representative at Ingram Micro, where she has been employed for 22 years.

Looking for a new road to travel, Shannon decided to pursue her lifelong desire to write her first book. She has always wanted to write fiction, but she felt she had a story to tell. Shannon's first book was released December 1, 2010. "My Reflection in the Mirror" is a look at some personal demons that she had to overcome. She hoped by telling her story she would inspire and empower other women.

October 4, 2013, Shannon lost her son, Brian, in an automobile accident. This was a devastating tragedy, but instead of sinking into a dark place, Shannon grieved and relied on her faith and trust in God. She began helping other parents that have lost a child. She started the Buffalo Chapter of Bereaved Parents of the USA. She also published her second book, "The Shattered Mirror: Picking up the Pieces." This book was about how she copes with the death of her son.

Because she felt that both these books were her personal testimony, she combined both books and published them as one. In 2018, she gave the book a face-lift with a new book cover and title: "Tribulation to Victory: Birth of a Queen." Shannon has several other books under her belt.

She is also the CEO and Founder of SMS Write On Publishing, LLC and SMS Film & Media, LLC. Shannon is a former board member for the William-Emslie YMCA and Our Curls, Inc. She is also the convener of the Faith Missionary Baptist Church Women's Christian Fellowship Ministry. In March 2018, she received the award, "Women Touching the World", for her community work. With all of these responsibilities, writing remains one of her top priorities, second to serving God.